INSIDER ONE

THE GOOD AND FAITHFUL SERVANT

Anthony Masters

Constable · London

First published in Great Britain 1999
by Constable & Company Limited
3 The Lanchesters, 162 Fulham Palace Road
London W6 9ER
Copyright © 1999 Anthony Masters
The right of Anthony Masters to be
identified as the author of this work
has been asserted by him in accordance
with the Copyright, Designs and Patents Act 1988
ISBN 0 09 478820 0
Set in Palatino 10 pt by
SetSystems Ltd, Saffron Walden, Essex
Printed and bound in Great Britain
by MPG Books Ltd, Bodmin, Cornwall

A CIP catalogue record for this book
is available from the British Library

To my dear friend Helen English whose tireless
and inspired work makes everything possible.

PROLOGUE

Eric had been working on Sand City for the entire morning. As the tide went slowly out he enlarged the boundaries, extended the moat and broadened the existing driftwood drawbridge with another miniature plank of damp, gnarled, seaweed-encrusted pine.

Inside the high sandy wall were clusters of spires and towers, moulded carefully from the wet mud on Margate beach. A turreted Gothic castle rose from a central square while narrow streets with less defined buildings spiralled outwards. Nearby was a huge and delicately sculpted cathedral, a number of churches and chapels, a small fort, a palace, elaborate gardens and a seaweed river. To the east lay the port with its ancient jetties; to the west a parade ground, scattered with Eric's limited collection of toy soldiers; to the north a tall lighthouse, and to the south an observation tower, the highest building in the city, where careful watch was kept for invaders, enemies and spies.

There was one invader, however, who was all-powerful and much feared: the Monster Child with snotty nose, rancid breath and malignant eyes, intent on destruction, dark silky hair blowing in a chilly wind.

'Mum!' Eric ran up to Vi in desperate appeal as she knitted away in her deckchair, huge legs burnt red, varicose veins like skeins of knotted cord. 'Don't let Andy wreck Sand City.'

'He's only a baby.' His mother gave him the gentle smile that, even at seven, Eric noticed never reached her eyes. 'He doesn't *mean* to do any harm.'

But Auntie Liz was already on her feet, shouting at the enemy who plodded forward with all the narrow focus of a five-year-old. Then she turned to Vi. 'Do something. You know he won't listen to me.'

But Andy just kept on coming and Vi's smile widened.

The walls were first to be crushed under his flip-flops. The observation tower was soon to follow. Seconds later Sand City was in an advanced stage of demolition.

'I hate you!' yelled Eric. 'I hate you, Andy.'

'Don't you speak to your brother that way.' Vi rose from her deckchair like a huge avenging angel.

As the enemy continued to trample civilisation, Vi clipped Eric round the ear.

He stood back, gazing down at the remains of Sand City, and Elizabeth sank back in her deckchair.

Eric never cried. Instead he began to hunt for his toy soldiers.

Part One

DANNY

1

'Not so fast.'

Danny was hardly listening for Abbie spoke more out of habit than anxiety.

'Go for it, Dad.' Rik was equally predictable.

'Listen to Mum.' Mary completed the ritual pattern of family nagging.

Danny Boyd drove on, his speed slightly increasing as he passed the Heathrow exit off the M25. They were travelling to St Albans for lunch with the Hadlows, and he had made himself late because he didn't want to go. Geoff played golf; Ann played bridge and their sons played rugby. When they weren't talking sport, their political views were somewhere right of Genghis Khan.

Traffic was light and Danny knew he'd better make the most of the magical moment for the M25 could seize up any second; bunching, failed lights on a spur road, a breakdown, a minor accident – any of those could bring the circulation to a grinding halt, holding them up for what seemed like an eternity on tarmac that would shimmer in the heat haze while his headache took on all the rigour of a fiery furnace.

Put your foot down, Danny told himself. The combination of a tailback *and* the Hadlows would be renewed torture. Geoff would be bound to offer sanctimonious advice in delighted hindsight. 'Look, old boy, if only you'd remembered to come off at Junction 18, you could – '

'Show us what you can do, Dad.' Rik wanted to wind up his sister – and mother too, if possible. That would be a high score indeed. 'It's the fast response stuff we need.'

'I'm desk-bound now,' Danny reminded his son.

Rik wasn't having any of that. 'Bomb it,' he commanded. 'Why don't you take that Peugeot? He's shit.'

'Shut up, Rik,' yelled Mary.

'And don't speak that way,' reproved his mother.

Rik scowled. He was going through his statutory rebellious

early teenage phase and he needed plenty of practice. 'Show us what you're made of, Dad.'

Danny accelerated, passing the Peugeot.

'Nice one,' said Rik approvingly.

He felt guilty pleasure at his son's praise.

The Boyds had only just moved into their new home in Sutton, and Danny felt deserved self-satisfaction. No more semis with regimented lap-top gardens. Of course, there were still improvements to make and Abbie had expansionist plans for the conservatory he was pretending he couldn't afford, although he was secretly savouring the pleasure of giving in to her.

After all, they'd finally made it, hadn't they? Rik at Kingston Grammar, Mary at Tiffins, Abbie a partner in the estate agents. Then there was his own promotion. Danny had never thought Glover would take early retirement, not even with his angina. But the old bastard had suddenly taken the plunge and Danny was on top of the world, king of the prairie, lord of the M25.

What he particularly liked about their new mock gabled house, The Oaks, was the summerhouse under the oak tree by the pond which smelt of creosote and fertiliser. He'd been pottering about there a good deal recently, making plans – a luxury Danny had never been able to afford while he clawed his way up the Met. Of course, he mustn't be complacent. He had to be continuously vigilant about the divisional crime rate, and there was still dead departmental wood to cut out. Danny wouldn't enjoy that. He wasn't ruthless enough.

'Slow *down*!' Abbie's voice was more than usually tight and he checked the speedometer. Nearly seventy so they were just within the limit, but he dropped back a little all the same.

She was often on edge now. 'It's all going too smoothly, isn't it?' she had said last night.

'What do you want?' he had asked her. 'World War Three? Armageddon? We deserve some upgrading, don't we?'

He had felt almost bitter about Abbie's anxieties. Couldn't she try to switch off for a while? After all, she loved The Oaks and the move from Kingston hadn't been that traumatic. Smooth even.

She kept saying how lucky they were. But it *wasn't* luck, that's what made Danny so indignant. Luck wasn't in it. He'd worked for this for so long, and now he'd been promoted they *should* have the good life. It was an award that mustn't be questioned, or put down to fortune smiling benignly on them.

He began to add up the plus factors. They loved each other and he'd never looked at anyone else. They'd been childhood sweethearts, and now here they were, in their mid-forties, with two talented teenage kids. Where had all the time gone, Danny suddenly wondered.

Was Abbie feeling that too? Was that why her sporadic nagging had developed an edge? Did they have something to talk about? Had they grown over-familiar with each other? Could they be heading towards some kind of mid-life crisis?

Of course they were too busy; what with his golf and Abbie's tennis, Rik's rugby and Mary's hockey, the Boyds didn't have enough time for themselves. Did she think they were getting too like the Hadlows? Surely, no one could possibly think they had any similarity to those farts, could they?

He caught a glimpse of the kids in the rear-view mirror. Rik with his square chunky build – just like his own, with the same shock of blond hair. Abbie and Mary were taller, red-heads with pale skin and a slight sprinkling of freckles.

Danny tried to banish his uneasiness by musing over the new furniture they had bought for the sitting room. Stylish, not Laura Ashley like the bloody Hadlows, but elegant, simple, blending with the wood floor. There were photographs, but not too many, authenticating the children as they grew up, in school uniform and sports gear. There were some of Danny with his golf-clubs, Abbie with her tennis racket and a couple of shots of the Costa del Sol, just to prove they had foreign holidays, focused on deckchairs, crowded beaches and pedalos. Sea, sun, sand and sangria. And sex of course, grunting behind painfully thin walls, hoping the kids weren't listening and wouldn't make fun of them the next morning.

Despite the hazards, however, he and Abbie still made it and didn't need, like a colleague, a stimulating dildo to bring on the action.

But recently, over the last few months, Danny had noticed a new rhythm to their lives that seemed slightly automatic.

Was it all too calculated? He recognised the mood swing, the questions, the unexpected indecision, feelings that had been with him all his life. Sometimes they surfaced like a shark, tearing his confidence to pieces.

A successful career, yes, but never a wholly certain approach. They were both lower middle born and bred and had met at a Young Conservative dance in Richmond. Couldn't be safer or more solid. Of course, Abbie had never liked him being in the Met, particularly in his younger days. But now he had an office carpet and rarely got his hands dirty on a villain or vice versa.

'You *are* going too fast, Dad,' complained Mary.

'Shut up!' sneered her brother. 'You wimpess you.'

'Don't start.' Abbie sounded drained.

'Sorry.' Danny glanced again at the speedometer and saw it was pushing ninety. 'Hadn't noticed.'

'And you a copper,' she reproved tolerantly, with a motherly, lightly disapproving tone.

Danny pulled back into the middle lane.

'Chicken,' said Rik.

'Shut it!'

Another status symbol the Boyds had earned in their unexpected upward mobility was Tiril from Trondheim, although her rugged Norwegian charm was rather lost on the kids. Abbie found the strapping ice maiden useful, Danny supposed, but all he could think about was her big arse that so regularly turned him on. Sometimes Danny wished Tiril would go home.

Now his mind was on mounting that big arse and he wondered again if he had really reached male menopause. Tiril this and Tiril that. Tiril fucked by a right old prat. The banal rhythm beat in his head. Cautious wet dreams were enough. The only twinge – and twinge it was – of disloyalty was that he saw Tiril when he was having sex with Abbie.

'What are you grinning at?' she asked.

'Geoff's face when he hears my handicap.' Did he sound too glib?

'We won't stay long, will we?' asked Mary.

'Until after tea.'

'That *is* long, Mum.'

'We've come a long way.'

'I don't like Henry,' complained Rik. 'He's a wanker.'

'And John's so selfish and horrible,' put in Mary, united with Rik for once.

Never mind, thought Danny as a wave of anger suffused him. Never bloody mind. Why couldn't the kids co-operate for once?

'Why are we going, Mum?' asked Rik aggressively.

'Because Ann's my cousin. She likes to see us.'

'We've already seen them twice this year.'

'Look,' Danny intervened, the anger sparking again, 'why don't you two try to do something for *us* for a change?'

'We have,' said Mary indignantly.

'What?'

'We tidied our rooms last night.'

'Is that all?'

'It took a long time.'

'That's because those rooms were tips,' said Abbie. 'You hadn't put anything away since we moved in.'

'Do you fancy Tiril, Dad?' Rik asked innocently.

There was a very brief uneasy silence, followed by hearty, liberated adult laughter which went on far too long.

'Don't be so *silly*, Rik.' Abbie still sounded amused.

Danny put his foot down on the accelerator. This time no one seemed to notice.

'*Do* you fancy Tiril?' Rik persisted, but his voice was more timorous the second time round.

'There's only one woman I fancy,' Danny reminded him, trying to lose the anger. 'And that's your mum.'

Rik made a derisory noise.

'Slow down,' said Abbie.

'Fucking speed up,' advised Rik.

Danny's anger hardened. 'If I ever hear you speak like that again, Rik, you'll be gated for a month.'

There was a sullen silence.

'Do you hear me? And that means the match.'

'You can't do that.' Rik sounded apprehensive and Danny felt a surge of triumph. They were beginning to compete against each other like stags locking antlers and he had the feeling that this instinctive rivalry was going to increase.

15

'Just watch me.'

'All right,' said Abbie. 'Let's talk about something interesting for a change.'

The tyre blew as she spoke.

The noise was like a gunshot and the Rover immediately veered into a skid.

'For Christ's sake!' Danny said to himself, but he only felt mild surprise as he watched the truck looming up out of nowhere on the sunlit motorway. He twisted the steering wheel but there was no response.

He felt as if the Rover was floating in a strangulated silence. Then they hit the truck.

The car seemed to momentarily take flight, shaking off the truck, hitting the barrier. Danny watched the radio and cassette disintegrate in slow motion, the sun visors spiralling away from him, the front storage compartment flying off.

Then, with a grinding and crunching of metal, a red veil hazed the windscreen until it blew out in diamond fragments and Danny watched the world of the Rover disintegrate. He felt almost curious as to what was going to happen next.

There were several more impacts and then something hit him hard in the face. Metal screamed, sparks showered and glowed, Rik's personal stereo flew over his head and Danny's seat seemed to rise up and then collapse beneath him. He felt no pain.

Eventually the rending sounds stopped and there was a deep wall of silence.

The roof was so compressed that Danny's head was pushed hard up against it, the dashboard resting on his chest. Come on, nightmare, he said to himself. Don't stay around too long. Let's get back to normality, even if that means being incredibly late for the Hadlows. There was a warm dampness on his head and in his lap.

He tried to turn, but pain suddenly, unexpectedly, moved in him like fire.

Danny looked down at the bloodied ball that had lodged in his lap. When he began to scream, the terrible noise seemed to be coming from someone else.

2

The white wall glinted and began to flash, and he covered his eyes as something he thought might be a curtain was pulled across. He glimpsed a pattern of tulips and the first verse of a song came into his head.

> When it's spring again,
> We'll meet again
> With tulips from Amsterdam.

The lines kept repeating themselves as someone spoke quietly.
'Can you hear me, Mr Boyd?'
'Yes.' His voice was so weak that Danny could hardly hear himself.
'Is the light too bright?' He couldn't see properly. The woman's head was glinting like the wall.
Danny nodded.
'Is that better?' The glint was gone, replaced by a thick, wafting haze. 'You've been unconscious.'
'How long?'
'Three days.'
'What's the matter with me?'
'You're poorly.' She had to be a nurse. Surely no doctor would use that smug little word?
'Have I had a coronary?'
'A road accident.'
'Where's my wife?'
'She's here.' There was fractional hesitation.
'Where is she? Was she in the accident? Is she hurt? The febrile frenzy was swept away by exhaustion, a thick grey sponge in his head.
'She's here. In the hospital. You're not strong enough to talk now. I've come to give you an injection. You need sleep. That's the real healer. Plenty of sleep.'

'Where *is* she?' Danny tried to sit up but found he couldn't move. He was trapped in his own body.

'It won't be more than a pin-prick.' The nurse was rolling up his pyjama sleeve.

'I had this dream.'

'What was it?'

'I had a football in my lap.'

Days of pain and sleep and pain again. Voices came and went but Danny couldn't understand what they were saying. The initial effort at communication had drained him totally, but Abbie and Rik and Mary seemed to be near, and in his dream state he saw them gathered round his bedside, bickering away.

Moment by moment, all that Danny longed for was some kind of relief from the pain which never came. When he had an injection the agony receded a little and he was able to sleep, but directly he woke again he found the pain was back, biting at him, deeper each time, like some ravening animal that wouldn't let go.

Sometimes he thought about the mysterious football that had bounced on to his lap, but even this was beginning to seem comparatively unimportant. It had probably belonged to Rik. Could it have been a rugby ball? The muddy ovaloid. The phrase repeated itself over and over again until his head hurt and Danny couldn't focus and faces were a blur.

One day there seemed less dazzle.

'I can see better,' he told the nurse.

'I'll tell the doctor.'

'What's your name?'

'Ana.'

'How long have I been here?'

'Ten days.'

'What's the matter with me?'

'We thought you had brain damage but the scan was fine. There was some internal bleeding and fractured ribs and a broken pelvis. You've been in a lot of pain.'

'I still am.'

'You're having injections at the moment, but the doctor might consider a morphine pump. Then you can control the pain yourself.'

Fatigue swept Danny. The brief conversation had once again used up all his resources and he slept deeply.

He woke sweating and screaming, and a different nurse came and gave him an injection. She was tall, angular and slightly horse-faced. His mother would have called her handsome.

'I keep dreaming about a football.'

'Are you kicking it?'

'I'm holding it.'

'You've had a touch of pneumonia but Dr Landis is pleased with you.'

'Good for him.' The pain seemed to have retreated to a more bearable threshold, but he knew it was only the injection and wondered how quickly the effects would wear off. Could the dose be increased? And if not, what was to be done? What about the morphine pump that no one mentioned any longer? He couldn't take much more.

But Danny felt too drowsy to pursue the vital question.

He lost all sense of time again. Sometimes he would wake and attempt to swallow his liquid diet, but soon he would drift back into unconsciousness. It was as if he was enchanted and had become the sleeping policeman.

Then the enchantment came to an abrupt and unpleasant halt.

'Your brother's here to see you.'

Danny surfaced. The nurse's voice had been slightly agitated as she pulled the tulip curtain round the bed.

He gazed up at Phil whom he had never liked yet who was now, after their parents' deaths, his only relative. He was a PE teacher, tall, sandy-haired, nondescript.

He sat down and crossed his long legs, but his knee hit the bed and he uncrossed them again.

'I've been in several times.' Phil's voice was thin and worn out from shouting at kids. 'But you've been out of it.'

'The pain's been bad. It's better now.'

'I'm glad about that.'

Cold dread suddenly knotted in Danny's stomach. He rarely saw Phil. Why was he here? It wasn't Christmas, was it?

'So what's new?'

'I've got something to tell you.' Phil cleared his throat in a way that had irritated him for years. A sort of 'ahem' that was sticky with phlegm.

'What is it?'

'The hospital thought it best –'

'Get to the fucking point!' Suddenly Danny realised how much the pomposity of this gawky bastard of a brother had always got to him. His slow thinking, his lack of imagination, the long-drawn-out stories, the seemingly wilful hesitation.

'Take it easy –'

'I *said*, get to the fucking point.'

'Try and –'

'Now!'

'Abbie . . .'

'Yes?'

'Very sadly, she's . . .'

'Dead,' Danny finished for him. But as he spoke the loss filled his mind with immense desolation and the shock waves broke through his muzziness, making the room, and especially the tulip curtains, ultra bright with a menacing clarity. It couldn't be true. She couldn't die. She couldn't leave him alone. But he knew, at the same time, that she had.

'I'm sorry.' Phil's beaky nose had some hairs sprouting from the nostrils and one particularly long one seemed to uncoil.

'Where are the kids?'

'They've gone too. I'm sorry, Danny.'

'Gone? Fucking gone where?'

He began to sob and was then seized by a rage he was too feeble to express. The rage was greater than the grief.

Phil sat awkwardly beside him, his eyes averted. After a while he said woodenly, 'They didn't suffer. The police told me they all died instantly. They wouldn't have known anything.'

Danny saw the football and knew what it was. The rage gave way to incredulity and then to nausea.

'What happened to her?'

21

'To who?'

'To Abbie.'

Phil stared at him.

'Answer the question.'

'I've no idea.' He got up. 'You need rest. I won't – '

'Answer the fucking question.'

There was a long silence during which Phil looked as if he wanted to run to the ends of the earth and then keep on running.

'Please, Phil.'

He was desperate to get away. 'You'll let me know if you need anything, won't you, Danny? Now you're perkier I'll drop in again tomorrow.'

The word 'perkier' seemed obscene.

'Did she lose her head?'

'Sorry?'

'Was she decapitated?'

Phil nodded and walked briskly towards the door. Then he abruptly returned.

'What about your au pair?'

'What about her?'

'Shall I pay her off?'

'And send Tiril back to Trondheim? Don't forget to give her a quick fuck before she goes. It would liven both of you up.'

With a glazed smile, Phil finally made his exit.

Abbie with her tennis and new house, stylish furniture and colour schemes had been careless enough to lose her head. Or rather he had been careless enough to lose it for her.

The football bounced and bounced again.

Danny began to vomit over the pristine sheets of his newly made bed and a nurse raced towards him, holding a bowl aloft as if it contained a libation to the gods.

'Did he tell you?' asked Ana.

'Yes.'

'I wish I could have done that, but it's meant to be the next of kin. He didn't look very comfortable.' Her English wasn't up to the subtlety of grief, but Danny knew what she meant. Phil wasn't a very comfortable person anyway.

'I don't feel anything,' he told her.

'You're in shock.'

Danny was grateful to her. She hadn't given him a single platitude.

He woke in the night to such pain that he began to scream, calling out their names, knowing the agony was no longer physical. Soon Ana was with him again, drawing the curtains, holding his hand as he sobbed like a child who had lost his parents rather than a man who had lost his family.

But despite the finality of their deaths, he recognised an unreality too, and whether he was asleep or awake, Danny could hear their voices as Abbie and Rik and Mary laughed, quarrelled and complained, so real he found it impossible to believe they no longer existed. At the same time, however, he understood the utter bleakness of their absence. The desert was inside him, cancelling out all thought, stretching to an unbearable infinity. The rage often returned, but directed at those he had loved so dearly for leaving him alone.

By the following morning, Danny's emotional trauma had outstripped, almost outsmarted his physical pain, and waiting for Ana to come back on shift was a deeply frustrating experience. When she eventually arrived he asked for the tulip curtains to be pulled around his bed.

'I have to see them.'

For once Ana was indecisive. 'I don't think that would be possible.'

'Why not?' Danny was as aggressive as his physical condition allowed. 'I've got to *know* they're dead. And the only way is to see them. Do you understand?'

'I haven't the authority.'

'Where are they?'

'They may have been taken away. I don't know. I'm sorry.' She paused, wanting to help, recognising the terrible need. 'Look – I'll try to find out.'

Danny took her hand. 'I'm grateful to you.' He wondered if he was going to cry but the tears wouldn't come. All he could feel was a huge kernel of pain, like a cancer, a dull ache that never let up.

Ana came back an hour later and pulled the tulip curtains round his bed.

Danny felt a bond between them. He also felt a curious excitement, as if, together, they might change the world.

'What did you find out?'

'They're still here.'

'How can I see them?' Danny suddenly realised he hadn't even got out of bed yet. He didn't know if he could stand, let alone walk.

There was a long silence during which he didn't want to interrupt, knowing she was trying to make up her mind. Inside, Danny prayed for the miracle she might bring him.

'I could take you in a wheelchair.'

He gazed at her searchingly, wanting to be perceptive, knowing that he had to be responsible for her. Or at least go through the motions. 'They haven't agreed, have they? You could lose your job.'

She shrugged and Danny was amazed at her easy ability to take such a risk.

'Aren't you studying here?'

'Yes.'

'You've got a lot to lose.'

'I'm homesick.'

'You'd be prepared to go back in disgrace?'

'I want to help you.'

'What about authorisation?'

'I might find a way.'

'Why are you doing this?'

'We honour the dead in our country,' she said simply. 'We don't lock them out of sight.' Some of the tension drained away and Danny felt his eyes weakly closing.

With a huge effort he managed to say, 'If you're sacked, you won't get references.'

Emotionally exhausted and hoping he had done his duty, Danny slid back into sleep.

*

Next day, enlisting the staff nurse's support, he insisted on trying to get up, and the request, referred to the doctor's round, was approved. They obviously admired him for making such stalwart attempts at recovery.

Trying to conceal the intensity of unbearable pain, Danny dragged himself out of bed and took a few steps with the help of a couple of nurses, one on either side, the sweat dripping off him until he could manage no more.

He returned to bed and slept until lunchtime. Towards four he tried again, this time with Ana alone, and managed eight paces before the deadening exhaustion and pain returned.

Sitting on the edge of Danny's bed, she whispered. 'I've spoken to the mortuary attendant.'

'Yes?'

'Your visit is OK.'

'That's unbelievable.' Danny looked at her suspiciously, and Ana smiled.

'I told him the doctor had given permission.'

'Won't that mean getting him to sign one?'

'I signed one for him.'

'Christ!'

'If I take you to the mortuary about ten, the attendant will let you see them – if that's what you still want.'

'I keep hearing them, seeing them. They won't let me sleep. They won't let me go.'

'You won't be able to see your wife,' Ana said hesitantly.

'Because of the condition of her body?'

She nodded.

'I can see the children?'

She nodded again, and this time, Danny felt tears pricking at the back of his eyes.

He didn't know how he was going to spend the rest of his life. The stark simplicity of the question was devastating. Should he live it at all? All he had in the world was Phil, and he wasn't exactly life-affirming.

Of course, there was the job and close camaraderie at the Met, but although Danny could imagine burying himself in work he still had to return to an empty house and the terrible poignancy of all the hopes and plans invested in The Oaks.

He contemplated the options open to him. Suicide was an attractive idea; an overdose, a slow, painless drifting into nothing. He had never been a religious man; he didn't believe in the after-life. Abbie, Rik and Mary were all he had had and in a moment of carelessness he had thrown them away.

The thought of that crass and monumental act of stupidity made the welcome adrenalin of rage rise, but his weakness quickly snuffed it out, and sleep came again, blotting out the enormity of what had happened – what was still happening.

In his dreams, the football bounced over the muddy field pursued by Danny and Mary and Rik. 'Wait for us,' came the childish voices on the raw wind. 'Wait for us, Mum.'

He was woken to a visitor.

'Who is it?'

'Superintendent Creighton. Are you feeling strong enough?'

Danny knew he wasn't. 'I'll see him.'

Creighton was a tall, slightly stooping, academic-looking man with half-moon glasses. The expression on his long narrow face was inscrutable but he had a quiet authority that was unexpectedly comforting.

'I'm deeply sorry.'

Danny had not seen much of his new boss. In fact, they were virtually strangers. Creighton had only met Abbie on one official occasion and had never seen the kids. Danny was glad of that.

'They tell me you're expected to make a full recovery.'

He didn't bother to reply.

'But you don't want to?'

'I'm not enthusiastic,' he admitted.

Creighton allowed a silence. Then he said, 'I know you will think I'm insultingly premature, but in your grief I want you to mull something over.'

'What is it?'

'No one can really know what you're going through, least of all myself. But we don't want to lose you.'

'What have I got to live for?' For a moment he wondered if his boss, with all his authority, could supply some miraculous

26

solution. Like cancelling what had happened in a God-like way, giving him a second chance.

Creighton gazed at Danny and then spoke with refreshing candour. 'Personally I don't think time does heal. It can only soften maybe. I often wonder if the dead – the dearest dead – become part of us.'

Strangely, Danny found Creighton's words helpful, but once again he didn't reply.

'Suppose you became someone else for a while?'

Was this visit actually happening, or was he still living in the unconscious?

'We're increasing the number of insiders we have in the Met. Obviously, an undercover agent has to take on a complete change of identity. I'm told it's rather like growing a new skin. There've been precedents, rather similar precedents, so that's why I took the risk of visiting you.'

'I become somebody else?'

'With a precise history that would be devised for you by an expert. You would have to forget your past and take on a new identity, tailor-made for the job.' Creighton paused. 'The role would be temporary, but it might give you a breathing space.'

'What *is* this job?'

'Too early to say.'

'So you prey on the bereaved?'

'There are other sources.' He gave Danny an ironic smile and shrugged. 'Do you have anyone else who is close to you?'

'A brother. I wouldn't say we were close.'

'He could be told you were working abroad. So could your friends and acquaintances.'

'There's always Tiril. Tiril from Trondheim.'

'I'm sorry . . .'

'The au pair. I'm told she's been in to see me a couple of times but I was asleep. Maybe she gave up. Anyway, my brother's dealing with her.'

'Is that going to work out?'

'He's very thorough.'

There was no doubt that Creighton was real, alive and well, flesh and blood, gazing over the top of his spectacles at him gravely. It was what he was saying that was unreal. Creighton almost seemed to be offering to spirit him away, just as Abbie and Rik and Mary had been. Then Danny had a thought, which swiftly grew in size and importance. If he agreed to these extraordinary demands, he might be able to postpone going home.

'I'm not asking for a commitment right now and you're going to be here for a while anyway.' Creighton spoke so casually that he sounded as if he had asked Danny to enter an inter-departmental golf tournament.

'If I did – take this job – where would I go when I leave here?'

'To a nursing home.'

'And then?'

'You'd work with a psychologist until he was satisfied you had completely absorbed your new identity.'

'What would happen to Danny Boyd?'

'He'd be on hold.'

'For how long?'

'As long as it takes.'

'What about my house?'

'We'd rent it out.'

'Who to?'

'Someone we can trust.' Creighton cleared his throat. 'Once your new identity is established, we might want you to work yourself into a family who've been involved in organised crime for generations. The big advantage of an insider is that he or she can break into an old-established network like it's never been broken into before. We don't want petty crooks, we only want the key players. The problem about them is that they're often working in isolation, pulling strings, pressing buttons, operating cells. Insiders can flush them out.'

'What's the result rate?'

'If agents survive, they can bring down empires. That's what we want. If they fail, they're dead meat.'

Danny was exhausted now and his eyes kept closing, yet he had surprised himself by his new-found stamina.

Creighton stood up. 'I've worn you out, so I'll come and see you again next week.' He gazed at Danny reflectively. 'Naturally, there's no pressure. If you don't want to go ahead, we'll just both assume this conversation didn't take place.'

If only the same could be said for what had happened on the motorway. In Danny's mind, the football bounced mockingly.

He slept again until Ana woke him, and as he struggled back to consciousness, he could scarcely believe that Creighton had been sitting by his bedside, offering him oblivion.

'Are you ready?' She had brought a wheelchair. 'You're meant to be visiting an old friend with a broken leg in Laburnum Ward. That's as near to the mortuary as I can get.'

Wasn't this a sign? A portent? He was going undercover already in his attempt to reach the corpses of his children.

'What did the sister say?'

'She thought you should do whatever you can to promote your own recovery – and seeing an old friend, even at this time of night, was fine by her. But she wants you back in forty-five minutes, so we can't be long. Can you manage to get into the wheelchair?' She glanced at him conspiratorially, and Danny felt a rush of affection for her.

Together they worked at the hell of his transfer into the wheelchair, gasping and sweating, the pain in his ribs so bad he could hardly breathe.

'OK?'

'I'll have to be.'

They passed the nursing station to muted encouragement, and in the soft, shaded light the nurses' faces seemed to romantically resemble medieval nuns, calm, icon-like. Danny felt as if he was floating, almost slipping away, already deidentified.

Ana pushed him towards the lift, her ebony arms lustrous in the subdued light.

As the door slid open soundlessly. Danny felt as if he was ascending to a hi-tec and glossily sanitised heaven.

The mortuary was on the fourth floor, approached via a number of rubber doors, finally leading to a steel shutter.

'Do you still want to go ahead?'

'I haven't changed my mind.'

'And you know you won't be able to see your wife.'

Danny thought again about the football and couldn't believe

it could be associated with Abbie. Instead he felt an unlikely sense of peace, of looking forward to being with loved ones.

Ana pushed a button, dialled a code on the security display, and the shutter opened soundlessly.

A stainless steel table stood in the middle of the sleek white space with one wall occupied by what looked like a giant filing cabinet. The atmosphere was sterile, with a generating hum Danny usually associated with refrigerators.

A young man in blue overalls strolled out of his office, dark hair pinned down under a cap. Ana gave him a document and he nodded apathetically, strolling over to his giant filing cabinet and pulling out a drawer.

'Your son's face is unmarked,' he said casually and clinically, as if he was standing at a supermarket counter, rejecting bruised fruit.

Danny's first impression was that Rik wasn't there. His eyes were closed, hair slightly tousled, features composed. He detected the small scar just above his eye, caused by a fall from his bike. There was another on his chin, the result of being kicked in a rugby match.

A white bandage ran across the back of his head, but apart from that there was no sign of any injury. Rik seemed to be a waxwork dummy, a good likeness but not himself at all. Danny's son, his real son, had gone away.

He propelled the wheelchair closer and leant out at an awkward angle to touch Rik's cheek which was icy cold. He pulled back as if he had been stung and then tried again, this time stroking the frozen flesh, forcing his hand to remain in position.

'He isn't there,' Danny muttered as Ana squeezed his shoulder.

'That's what I thought when I saw my mother after she died. I said to myself, she isn't there. The spirit has gone.' She concluded abruptly, as if she thought she had been talking too much. 'Do you want to see your daughter? Apparently she's not – in such good shape.'

'No,' said Danny with sudden decision, as a familiar emptiness spread. He knew now that she wouldn't be there.

'You sure?' asked Ana quietly.

'Quite sure.'

Danny awkwardly turned the wheelchair away, glancing up at the attendant. 'Thanks very much.' He wanted to go now, to leave as fast as he could.

'Did it help?' Ana was flustered as she began to push him out of the gleaming white space that now seemed even more arid than before.

'Thanks,' he replied, as if she had just offered him a cup of tea.

When they arrived back in the ward after a silent journey, the night nurses had changed from idealised nuns to jovial harpies.

'Had a good time then? Nice-looker, is she?'

Ana wheeled Danny over to his bed as quickly as she could. She helped him out of the chair and between the sheets while the pain returned, lashing at him relentlessly.

'Shall I get you some relief?' she asked.

Not in this life, he thought. Then Danny remembered what Creighton had offered him. Wasn't that the antidote?

3

He lay awake, feeling unformed, floating, without purpose.

A nurse trod softly towards the fluttering breathing of an old man, someone called out in their sleep, a pager buzzed, the telephone rang, muffled and distant, a bedside light was switched on, there was whispering, stillness, then whispering again.

Danny sat up in bed as Ana appeared.

'Do you want a drink?'

'No.'

'How's the pain?'

'What's the time?'

'Just after two.'

'He wasn't there, was he?'

'No.'

'Like your mother. Why didn't you warn me?'

'I thought I had.'

When Ana had gone, Danny slept and dreamt vividly of childhood holidays in Swanage, a small seaside town in Dorset. He was sitting on the top step of a beach hut while the tide swirled beneath. The Boyds had always taken a fortnight here, waiting for the unpredictable sun, splashing in the cold grey-green water, gazing up at the overcast sky.

The Macfarlans with their brood of kids had taken the hut next door, while on the other side the Dawsons were in residence.

At twelve o'clock each morning the adults would tramp up the cliff path for a drink at the Grand Hotel, leaving their offspring ostensibly playing on the beach. In their absence, the play became different as they fondled each other. Danny went with Dawn. Phil with Alice. Phil's fumbling was brisk.

Danny would never forget the inside smell of seaweed and sandwich spread, but they did little beyond rubbing their bodies slowly together, knowing exactly what time the slightly tipsy guilty adults would return for the sand-in-the-sandwiches lunch. Five minutes before that deadline, if the tide was out, they would emerge self-consciously, over-enthusiastically joining in a game of beach cricket, the younger children, bribed with sweets, never mentioning what went on behind closed doors.

'I love you, Danny,' Dawn had said. 'I'll always love you, Danny.' She had used his name a lot when they were rubbing, as if she wanted to savour it. Danny. Danny. Danny Boyd.

The name – his own name – pounded in his head and pre-puberty eroticism aroused him again. Danny. Danny Boyd.

He woke weeping and sat up in bed to find Ana squeezing his hand tightly.

'What's happening?'

'You were dreaming,' she replied. 'Saying your name over and over again, as if you were frightened of losing it.'

'That's just what I want to do,' he muttered.

4

Fred Cole watched the small black and white TV set while his cell mate slept. They both had their separate ways of seeing the long prison day through.

As the screen flickered, his thoughts returned to their usual depressing track. At seventy, Fred was contemplating retirement. He looked older than he was, his face a mass of lines, his body scrawny despite the stodgy prison food. But even in his prison uniform of check shirt, blue trousers and slip-on shoes he still managed to look smart. Fred always shaved, always combed and oiled his glossy black hair, a crop that thrived, sleek and handsome, at odds with his gnomic body.

Retirement? What was he going to do? They had a nice house in Sunningdale, a nice house on the Costa Brava. The word 'nice' was synonymous in Fred's mind with money. A nice car was a Mercedes. A nice carpet was an Axminster. A nice malt was Glenlivet.

Not for Fred the crooked coastline of the Costa del Sol for he had no intention of rubbing shoulders with all that East End trash. Blanes was different. At least the place had a bit of class and he and Vi might spend more time there, the only problem being the intense heat. Made you lazy, resting all day, avoiding the nice sun, only going out in the cool of the nice evening. He'd have more scope at St Tropez, the nice Gothic in Sunningdale. Fred had always wanted to do something practical, although it was Vi who had the green fingers. Now his ambition was to build her a walled garden.

'Going to wall yourself up, Dad?' He could hear Eric's voice now. Handing over the business to him wasn't going to be easy – not with Vi feeling the way she did. Andrew would have been more than acceptable to her, but with only Eric left, she was resisting. More than resisting. Vi was refusing point blank. But to Fred the inclusion of his elder son was everything. He was family.

Vi had never made a secret of her attitude. Don't let Eric get his hands on a penny. She never could stand her adopted son. *His* son. But Fred was determined that there would be a Cole at the helm, just like his father before him.

He closed his eyes against the TV cookery programme, but really he was trying to avoid the grinding daily pressure of worrying about Eric. He had tried all kinds of distractions – even the meditation group in D Wing – but no amount of mantra chanting seemed to help.

Andrew had been dead from a heroin overdose for two years now, and Fred knew that Vi would never recover. She had never wanted Eric as a baby let alone a child, and nowadays insisted on seeing him as villain rather than victim. Fred sometimes wondered if this was her way of punishing their son for his father's mistake, but he chose not to confront her.

What really worried him more than anything else was the eventual clash of wills that could irretrievably damage both their marriage and the business. Fred and Vi had always had an understanding, a way of getting through. He had to take good care of that.

Vi had centred her life on Andy who had had all the family charisma. Tall, like Vi's own brother, his features hawkish and pale, he'd also inherited Fred's lustrous black hair.

Eric was short and heavy in build. He looked – and behaved – like the salesman he had once tried to be. Over-confident, relentlessly pushy, always having that one good laugh too many. But underneath there was an inadequacy, a raw jealousy that festered. Fred had tried to talk to him, but Eric hadn't wanted to listen. Not ever.

At the beginning Fred had been more hopeful, for surely good old Vi would bring Eric up as her own? But she hadn't. Instead, Vi had hired an Italian nanny and Maria had cared for Eric more than adequately, but it wasn't the same. He had needed a mother's love, an indefinable quality that Fred regarded as sacred. As a result he had begged Vi's forgiveness more times than he'd had hot dinners. But it was not to be.

She had only said, 'I love you, Fred, and I always will. So I'm no good in bed? I'll accept that too. But don't bring home any more of your little bastards and expect me to play Mum.'

Two years later, after Vi had miscarried three times and been told she'd never carry a baby to full term, Andy had been born, confounding the doctors. She had been ecstatic, and even managed to do a little better with Eric. Only a little though.

Now, thirty years later, Vi was insisting that the rumours were true and Eric was up to his neck in smuggling heroin through Gatwick airport. It didn't bear thinking about. Fred certainly wasn't going to believe the grapevine, was he? It was always tipped against success stories like the Coles. Bound to be. There were a lot of jealous bastards out there.

Fred and Vi never dealt in drugs. Protection, bent bookies, motor trade fraud, gaming scams and robberies were at the heart of their business. If Andy had been alive they would have been happy to retire, knowing he would run the old firm just as his loving parents would have wished.

Even now, the business was flourishing and Eric couldn't go wrong. Definitely hadn't gone wrong. Besides, if he was up to his neck in the shit, Eric would have told his old man. Fred was sure of that. They had always been open with each other.

Vi had been holding the reins while he had been inside – as she had done several times before – and, if she outlived him, Vi and Eric would work together and maybe that would bring them closer. But Fred was also certain she would fight him every inch of the way.

There was another factor which had been worrying him. Apart from Vi's prejudice against Eric, apart from the bitter disputes about the future, the business was ripe for picking. Takeovers in the South London underworld were usually rather more brutal than those on the stock market, and for the first time in a long while Fred had been shitting bricks. Midas had been watching the business with interest and approval. But Midas's approval was a noose.

Vi arrived at visiting time and Fred noticed once again how much weight his old girl had put on. Only that big, handsome face with those startlingly large blue eyes saved her from looking like the Incredible Hulk.

Her dependence on comfort food had become much more pronounced in the raw aftermath of Andy's death, and even now, two years later, the scoffing showed no sign of letting up. Vi had found Andy in the summerhouse, the tourniquet on his arm, his dead eyes seeming to still scrutinise a sunlit cobweb. Since then, she had been eating on such a vast scale that an explosion could be imminent.

Now Vi was sitting down at the other end of the table in the bleak room that smelt of damp mackintoshes. Fred could see that she was gasping for breath even after the small exertion of walking down a short corridor.

Suppose she scoffed herself to death? Was that possible?

'You've got to watch that weight, girl.'

She opened the packet of chocolate biscuits as if she hadn't heard him, pushing one over the table as a token gesture.

'Wednesday fortnight. You'll come and get me?'

'I've been thinking.' Vi's voice was deep, almost hoarse, roughened by a lifetime's smoking. Because of a cousin's lung cancer, she had finally got the message and given up. Even Andy's death had not induced her to begin again.

'What about?' He was wary at once.

'We'll need a driver. You've still got months off the road.'

In addition to his problems with the CID, Fred had also been breathalysed positively by the traffic police. A week after Andy's death he had been found sprawled across the front seat with his car half-way up the pavement. The ban had been imposed for three years.

'Keep taking the taxis.'

'We need a driver, Fred. Maybe a minder too.'

Vi crunched her way through another chocolate biscuit and this time she didn't offer him the packet.

'We've no need of that rubbish. We can look after ourselves.'

'You know we're in profit, Fred. You know as well as I do that Midas are taking a look. Might take a pop too.'

'If anything happened to us they wouldn't get a penny,' muttered Fred. 'I've sewn up my will.'

'What about an inside job? There's Mack for starters.'

'Not with Eric around.'

'He's more likely to open the gates.'

'Why don't you get off that boy's back?'

'You don't see. Your eyes are shut.' She started on another biscuit.

'You saying we need to protect ourselves against our own son?' Fred's voice rose.

'Keep your voice down, for Christ's sake.'

He leant across the table. 'You're talking shit, girl. You may have to eat it one of these days.'

'Eric thinks he's getting the business, doesn't he?'

'If I retired, you'd be partners. You know that's what I want.'

'And the more you want it, the more ambitious he gets. He could be in bed with Midas now.'

'Our own son?'

'Don't keep saying that, Fred. It gets boring.' She finished the last chocolate biscuit, wiped her mouth with a handkerchief and put the wrapping back in her handbag. 'That's why we need a minder.'

'Look, Vi. I know the boy through and through. He tells me everything.'

'He's up to his neck in shit,' she said impatiently. 'That's how we lost Andy. Eric turned him on.'

'Don't keep saying that, Vi.' Fred mimicked her voice. 'It gets boring.'

'Mother's intuition.'

'Bullshit!'

'Stop blustering, Fred.'

They were on the verge of another row.

'At the rate you stuff yourself, you'll have a coronary.'

She stroked his wrist before the screw could see her. 'Don't let's row, love. We won't see each other for another fortnight.' There was an uneasy silence. Then Vi said firmly, 'We're going to need someone to keep an eye on us.'

Fred looked away and she knew she had won.

'What you brought me?' he demanded.

'Chocolate.'

'Any left?'

'Don't be rotten.'

'You got someone in mind?'

'I've got me a prospect.' she said determinedly. 'Name of Pollard.'

'Never heard of him. What you doing? Scraping the barrel?'

'I went down the King's Head. Russell told me about Pollard. Small-time bragger. Been out in Cape Town.'

'Seen him?'

'Informally.'

'What about his cred?'

'He knows how to use a shooter.'

'This is well out of order, Vi.'

'Is it?'

'I don't like these times.'

'We've all got to adjust.'

'I was looking forward to getting home,' Fred said savagely. 'Now I've got a fucking minder under the bed.'

'Better than a bullet up your arse.'

5

'I've got another interview with Vi next week,' said Danny, sitting in the garden of a safe house in Somerset. The early spring sun was pleasantly warm, filtering the daffodils with faint rays through an old cherry tree.

'Think she'll bite?' Robin Farringdon, undercover section head, leant back in his chair, a large, crumpled man with a ginger beard and an impassive manner. Sean Pollard was Kieron Ray's creation, but Farringdon's responsibility.

'Yes.'

'What's the delay?'

'Fred. There seems to be discord.'

'Where would you live?'

'Over the garage.'

'Is there a predecessor?'

'Apparently not. So tell me more.'

'The Coles are at odds with each other over a lot of stuff.'

'Eric with the Gatwick connection?'

'That's one little problem.'

'And the other?'

'Success. Fred and Vi have the most lucrative criminal outfit in South London. Fred inherited from his dad. He would have liked to pass the business on to Andrew, but he died from a crack overdose. Neither of them ever got over that. Eric's the only one left now, but he's the wrong kind of villain for Vi. The Coles don't do drugs and, anyway, she reckons Eric turned Andrew on.'

'Who am I meant to be minding them from?'

'Other businesses? Their own? Eric? And there's always Midas.'

'What's that?'

'They've been around a long time.'

'I've never heard of them.'

'You wouldn't – not in the Met.'

'Thanks.'

40

'They're better known to Interpol – and us. Midas are a group of international financiers who fund terrorism and large-scale criminal activity – a kind of illegal monetary fund if you like. You've got to be big to get them interested.'

'Fred's as big as that?'

'He had a good few years financially – if not personally. But there's only one problem with Midas. They offer "advice" to up and coming businesses, loans for expansion – that kind of thing, but it's not unknown for them to be hands-on. Like squeezing hard. There's been a real scourge of gangland killings recently. The Coles are feeling insecure.'

'So they could take them over?'

'They could wipe them out. If they get the right opportunity. There's been a detectable crack in Cole solidarity. Vi doesn't want Eric to inherit, but the grapevine claims Fred does. Ideal dilemma for the Midas touch.'

'What kind of guy is Eric?'

'Interests in the motor trade, couple of dealerships, car hire, and that's about it. But he's not that solvent.'

'So he needs a little fluidity. What about Gatwick?'

'Crack's arriving in the UK on routine passenger flights from the Far East and Europe which gets seen through. We want to define Eric's role.'

'If the run's efficient, how come you know so much?'

'Informer. Works as a baggage handler. I've interviewed him myself.'

'You were satisfied?'

'Not entirely. He told us just so much – enough to whet the appetite. Then he did a runner.'

'Looks like they sussed him.'

'So it's going to be a long job. How do you feel about Sean Pollard then?'

'He reminds me of being a kid on a French exchange. I remember how it put me on a high reading a book in English at night. Speaka their lingo all day and bask in your own at night. Except that's just what Kieron's told me not to do. I've got to be Pollard through and through. Boyd's dead. Like his family.'

Farringdon said nothing, his hands clasped in front of him, but in his eyes Danny could see a full understanding of his position, in all its grim reality.

41

'Where does your brother think you are?'

'Australia. I wrote all the letters in advance – like I did to the Met.'

'The new hairstyle works.'

'Not to mention this little close-cropped beard. I still get one hell of a shock when I look in the mirror. It's rather as if I've been stolen by the fairies.'

'Your closest friend – even your brother – wouldn't recognise you,' said Farringdon.

'That's reassuring.'

'Your main objective is to find out whether Eric Cole's involved in the Gatwick ring – or not. You only get a micro tape, and that's got to be used sparingly. We don't want to use a tracker because they've been discovered on an insider too often and the cover's blown. You'll just have to use good old-fashioned human faculties, ineffective as they often are.'

'How do I contact you?'

'We'll do that.'

'Without a tracker? Or are we into mind-reading?'

'Alas, we haven't been sufficiently elevated. Yet. So we'll do the tracking. Now, there's one other thing. You've had small arms training?'

'Way back.'

'It'll have to do. We haven't got the time to retrain you.'

'Am I going to be armed?'

'Not by us.'

'By who then?'

'Vi Cole is a tough lady. If she needs that kind of protection, she'll see you're properly equipped. The old man's a pussy-cat but the old girl comes from a dying élite – honour amongst thieves. If you can get her to trust you then we're all in with a chance.'

'What does she want? A bent Boy Scout?'

'Just someone who's up to snuff. I think she has this big worry about what's going to happen when Fred gets out.'

'Midas?'

'Them – and other possibilities.'

Part Two

SEAN POLLARD

6

Sean went for a walk in a South London park. The bulbs were almost over, waiting for the gardeners to come and remove them, and the grass was thin and muddy. The basin of an ornamental fountain was dry and buried deep in noxious litter.

Inside Sean, Danny lurked, ready to destroy the identity that Kieron had laboured so long to create.

'You have to live and breathe Sean,' he had told him. 'He has to be everything.'

'What happens when it's over?'

'You'll find you've shed a skin.'

'And Danny returns, grief still on hold?'

'There'll be less pain, more distancing. That's all you can expect.'

As Sean strolled down to the boating lake, he felt as if he was in limbo. He was nothing, belonged to no one, had become a stranger to himself. He also had yet to convince Vi Cole that he could be useful.

The water, moved by a light breeze, lapped against the concrete steps as a heron hovered and then dived. Then the bird rose, beak empty.

'I like your driving.'

Vi sat in the back of the black Mercedes that smelt of leather and linseed oil, eating a chocolate biscuit.

The dual carriageway was crowded with fast-moving traffic heading towards the M3, and Sean was desperate not to make the slightest mistake, particularly on his first morning. He didn't want to disappoint her now that she had finally decided to hire him. He also had a considerable problem driving, and if there was anything that was going to break his new identity that was it. Sean's greatest fear was that Vi would ask him to pass Junction 15 of the M25. That would be his ultimate test.

She had gone to considerable trouble to make him comfortable. The flat over the garage had been tastefully redecorated with Van Gogh yellow walls, basket chairs and low-slung black sofas.

Sean had expected her to be a vulgar old bat. 'Jumped-up', as his mum would have said. Then he had had to correct himself. He was thinking about his own mother not Sean's, which Kieron had so assiduously warned him against. 'If you think Danny, you're finished. You're bound to make a give-away slip or have a fatal moment of confusion. You've got to think Sean. All the time. Like I said – even when you're in bed at night.'

'I'd like to take a look at the river,' said Vi, breaking into the complex pattern of his thoughts. 'What about Runnymede then?'

Turning left off the roundabout, he refreshed his memory. 'Give yourself a mental briefing every day.' Again Sean rehearsed the scenario. Sean Pollard, born to John and Diana Pollard, 14 Stamford Rise, Clapham. Father owned a coach-works. Mother worked in the office. An only child brought up in a marriage that had gone sour but never ended in divorce, simply maintaining an arid, hopeless, loveless way of life. Sean had passed his eleven-plus and gone to the local grammar school, but he had soon gravitated to the 'wrong crowd' who were hard to find but once unearthed were more likely to cheat in exams than take and drive away, all heading for the gentler world of white collar fraud and open prisons.

Sean had been expelled for extorting money from younger boys and at sixteen had joined the Junior Leaders in the Royal Engineers. After a spell in Cyprus he had left the army and had just started work as a demolition contractor when his parents were killed in a road accident. 'That's to give you some powerful emotions to hang on to. Just so it's not all done by numbers,' Kieron had reminded him.

After a fight in a pub, Sean had left the UK for South Africa where he continued, less successfully, with the demolition con-tracting. He later degenerated into petty criminality, specialising in taking and driving away, then repainting and reidentifying stolen cars in partnership with a Spaniard, Juan Mantos. But there wasn't enough profit margin to make a proper living.

Later, Sean had met a prostitute, exotically named Eleanora Langerbilt. He had become her pimp and shortly afterwards her lover, and for the first time in many years achieved a certain street-wise stability. But not for long.

Eleanora turned out to prefer women's bodies to men's and Sean had soon found himself on the receiving end of ritual humiliation. He beat her up, was arrested and 'spotted' by the secret police as having the right 'qualities' for placing suspects under surveillance. When he had served out his usefulness, Sean was put on a flight to Heathrow and found himself fruitlessly job-hunting in London.

He had ended up living in a squat, turning up in Vi's local with many a tale to tell – tales that were listened to and registered by talent spotters of a different kind. Eventually, they came to Vi and told her that the 'prospect seemed authentic'. They added that Pollard had been 'out of it' for a long time. That, she had known, reduced the risk of a plant who, once accepted, would kill her.

As the spring sun came out, Sean drew up by a café on the banks of the Thames. Swans drifted past and the tables and chairs on the lawn that swept down to the river looked invitingly empty.

'Let's have a cuppa,' Vi heaved herself out of the Mercedes. She wore a blue two-piece with a striking floral print, and her big handsome face was wreathed in a hopeful smile. 'Wonder if they got any doughnuts?'

'I'll go and see.' Sean wore a dark suit, white shirt, a narrow knotted club tie and highly polished black shoes. He felt rather stagy, as if he was about to step on to the set of a drawing-room comedy to the cue line of 'Ring for the chauffeur.'

'Get me a couple then,' Vi called, settling herself in a stately pose on a green wooden chair that was only just capable of bearing her weight.

Doughnuts were not on the menu. Instead, Sean apologetically returned with two teas and a couple of slabs of desiccated-looking fruit cake.

Vi was disappointed. 'I just fancied a couple of them dough-nuts,' she muttered, fingering the fruit cake suspiciously.

'Oozing jam?' he asked.

'I want the jam in the middle – where it *should* be.'

'We could try somewhere else.'

'We haven't got time for a doughnut hunt, have we?' Vi gave Sean a motherly smile of approval. 'Think we'll suit, do you?'

'I hope so.'

She had finally come clean at the interview. 'Fred and I need looking after. For business reasons. You any good at that kind of lark?'

He had assured her that he was.

'Of course, we're pacifists. Do I take it you can find your own little shooter?'

Sean had told Vi that finding his own little shooter should present no problems, and with the kind of money she'd given him it certainly wasn't. All he'd had to do was to return to the squat and haggle a price that would leave him in profit. For a moment, Danny had surfaced, startled by the ease with which Sean had acquired his underworld familiarity, but he had been swiftly squeezed back inside his box, where he lay coiled, ready to spring. Sean had to be vigilant.

Vi gazed down at the swans gliding on the windless surface of the river. 'Nice and peaceful, isn't it? I want it to stay that way – particularly when Fred gets out.' She paused and Sean knew better than to interrupt. 'You're going to have to be on the ball all the bleedin' time. You know that, don't you?'

For the first time he detected anxiety.

'That's what I'm here for.'

'We never expected to need a minder.' Vi munched mournfully. 'This cake's shit.'

'Shall I take it back?'

'I'll manage. Good cup of tea though.' She sipped at it appreciatively. 'Nice and strong. Yours OK?'

He nodded, pleased by the companionship between them.

'What do you think of our place?' she asked.

'Terrific.'

St Tropez was red-brick Gothic, hidden behind a laurel hedge, like many of the more sumptuous houses in Sunningdale. Closely mown green lawns swept down to an ornamental lake, on which imitation ducks and even swans floated. Concrete cats

48

sat on the terrace and a stone dog crouched at the bottom of the steps to the imposingly arched front door.

'Can't stand animals,' she had told him on the first day. 'They make a mess.' Vi had stopped short, however, of garden gnomes. 'We've got a place on the Costa Brava too,' Vi continued. 'You'll be coming out there with us one of these days.'

Sean just stopped himself saying 'Terrific' for the second time. 'I'll look forward to that. Love a drop of sun.'

'You had that in Cape Town.'

'Not where I was. It was mostly blotted out by sea fog.'

She gazed searchingly at him for a few seconds, crumbs around her lips, some scattering down to her chin.

Sean wondered what she was thinking.

Vi got slowly to her feet, wheezing slightly.

'Nice spot.'

They walked back to the Mercedes.

'Time for lunch. Then I'll have a snooze.'

An Italian couple looked after the Coles. Roberto was in his sixties and had the distinguished look of a silver-haired diplomat. He was in charge of maintenance and the garden while his wife Maria did the cooking and cleaning, although she had originally been Eric's nanny. After being at St Tropez for so long they hadn't been pleased to see Sean, but he regarded their ill-concealed hostility as a bonus. There was no chance of unwanted companionship. The Corsinis had declared their own passive war of attrition.

Sean drove slowly back, keeping to the inside lane while the stereo played *The Three Tenors*, which he had discovered was Vi's favourite disc. In fact, she never allowed anything else to be heard.

'Do you think we're being followed?' she asked unexpectedly.

For a moment Sean wondered if Vi was paranoid. Then he saw the Ford Mondeo behind them in the rear-view mirror. The road was clear. Why didn't he overtake?

'Do you want me to lose him?'

'Just see what happens.'

'Is that a good idea?'

'I think so,' said Vi firmly.

She didn't want him to take the initiative.

Sean slowed down a little more and for a few seconds the Ford still kept pace with them. Then it accelerated and passed the Mercedes, the driver looking shrunken behind the wheel.

'That's either a very small person, or he kept his head well down.'

'What do you think then?' Vi seemed slightly shaken.

'I think I should be more alert,' said Sean, hoping that self-criticism would count.

'Don't worry. I'm beginning to take to you, Sean. I like a man who admits his mistakes. As long as he doesn't make too many.'

But when they got back to the house, Vi seemed depressed and went inside without speaking.

Sean drove the Mercedes into the garage, and then ran up the steps to his flat. He unlocked the door and went straight to the bedroom, flinging himself down on the divan, anxious to take a rest and then have a drink. He had been strictly rationing alcohol. Kieron had warned him against it. Bugger Kieron.

Then the internal telephone began to ring.

'Why don't you come over?' asked Vi. She suddenly sounded older.

Sean hurried to obey.

She was sitting in the upstairs lounge, surrounded by furniture that Sean couldn't believe had been incorporated without a sense of irony. Fake panelling gave way to fake bookshelves that slid aside to reveal a hi-tec cocktail cabinet and a Gaggia coffee machine. Deep pile carpet, Jacobean (fake) furniture, a Georgian (fake) fireplace and mantelpiece covered in dozens of photographs of a slightly built young boy growing up into a slightly built young man. There was something defensive about him.

Vi was sitting on a Victorian (fake) sofa with tassels, and Sean wondered how his own flat had escaped the Cole touch. Perhaps all this grandeur was down to Fred.

50

'Want a drink?' She had a large gin and tonic on the (fake) walnut coffee table in front of her.

'Something soft.'

'Forever cautious.' She sounded a little slurred and Sean was surprised at how much she had obviously packed away in such a short time. Vi got up, went to the cocktail cabinet and gave him an orange juice. She sat down again heavily. 'I been thinking.'

'Yes?'

'Fred's coming out in a fortnight.'

'I'm looking forward to meeting him.'

'He was dead against me employing you. But, of course, I know better, don't I?'

'I hope he'll find me useful.' He wondered how much of a threat Fred was going to be.

'You heard my son died of an overdose?'

He was startled by the sudden change of subject. Should he admit that he knew or not? Sean decided he would. 'Yes. I do know. I'm very sorry.'

'Everyone knows.' Her large blue eyes were on his, almost unwinking. 'Now, if you've heard about Andy, you're bound to have heard about Eric.'

The remark was equally loaded. What was he going to say now? What *would* he have heard on the grapevine? Once again, Sean knew he was going to have to take a risk.

'I heard there was some kind of rift.'

'You can say that again.'

'You don't speak?'

'Fred's close to him. But not yours truly.'

'One of my aunties didn't speak to my mum for thirty years, not till the day she died and then she practically spat at her.' Sean realised he was making up additional script, always a dangerous move in Kieron's view.

Vi permitted him an indulgent smile. 'I have to protect the business, you see.'

There was a long silence which Sean decided against breaking.

'Eric looks cocky enough, but underneath he's shitting bricks.' She paused. 'He's a crafty sod. I mean, he could have planted you, couldn't he?'

'Sorry?' This was getting worse.

51

'On a contract.'

Sean laughed too heartily and was instantly and painfully reminded of Rik asking, 'Do you fancy Tiril?' His voice was like a knife slitting Danny's flesh. 'You got my credentials,' he said.

'What credentials?' A little smile was playing at the corners of her mouth.

'A rank outsider.' The pain was slowly, relentlessly, engulfing him.

'You got your Cole protector?'

Sean pulled up his shirt to reveal the small automatic strapped to his waist.

'Looks like a toy.'

'It's a nasty one.'

'You got a nice firm body. What's that scar on your ribs?'

That was Danny's. And it was fresh.

'Had a bit of a kicking.'

'Looks recent.'

'It is.'

She didn't reply and drank more gin.

'Do you really think your son's a threat to you?' He needed to divert her attention.

'Yes, I bloody do, particularly with Fred determined to hand him the business on a fucking plate. It was his father's before him. A regular little dynasty. Now he wants Eric on board.' Vi got up and made herself another drink. 'It's what Eric's up to that worries me.'

'What is he up to then?' Sean sat back, trying to look relaxed, crossing one leg over the other, sipping at his orange juice. A sudden image of Phil came into his mind. What would he make of him now? The hair in his brother's nostril uncoiled again. 'This is a bad show,' he would have said.

'Stuff that his father and I wouldn't touch.'

'Drugs?' He wondered if he had gone too far.

'We're very out on a limb, Fred and I. We run the business together, but since he's been inside I've taken over the responsibility and I can tell you it gives me a lot of grief.' Vi lurched over to a French (fake) escritoire and took down what looked like the most recent photograph of Andrew, handing it to Sean. He could smell the gin on her breath and tried not to draw back as she placed a heavy hand on his shoulder. Does she make a habit of getting rat-arsed in the afternoon, he wondered, or was this just for him? He suddenly imagined her bulk straddling him commandingly. It was not a pleasant thought.

'He's handsome.' Sean was gazing down at the tall thin young man with his glossy black hair.

'He *was* very handsome.' Vi struggled for control, her voice even more heavily slurred now. 'Towards the end he lost a lot of weight. When he died he looked like he'd just come out of fucking Belsen.'

'You say Eric turned him on?'

'Of course he bloody did.'

Sean regretted the careless assumption. Had she told him that or hadn't she? He couldn't remember.

Vi put the photograph back on the escritoire. On her return journey to the sofa she stumbled and knocked over a small coffee table which Sean righted, taking a discreet look at his watch as he did so. It was only three in the afternoon. Could she be persuaded to go and take a siesta, or would she just collapse on the sofa and sleep it off?

Had the car Vi thought might have been following them upset her more than he had imagined?

'Were you ever close to Eric?' Sean risked asking.

Vi shrugged and drained her glass, heavily slumped on the sofa. Then she spoke, ignoring the question. 'They say he's running crack.'

'Isn't your husband worried by these rumours?'

'Fred's a bit of an optimist.' The bitterness was back.

Maybe I'm lucky to catch this side of her, thought Sean. He wondered if he should milk her just that little bit more. 'Can't someone give him a good slapping?'

There was a long silence and Sean wondered if he had finally blown it, but Vi seemed to accept the question as reasonable.

'They wouldn't fucking dare. That's our job. I keep a tight hold even if Fred doesn't. We're his parents, for Christ's sake.'

She got up with difficulty, swaying in a rather stately manner.

'I think I need a little siesta, dear. I don't usually drink in the day but I've not been myself. Go and get a drop of fresh air.'

*

53

As Sean walked out into the grounds, he was sure that he had asked too many leading questions and made a mental note to be more careful.

The lawns ran down to a lake and in the centre of a small island Sean could see a folly in the shape of a pagoda.

Rough woodland surrounded the grounds and there was no sign of any fencing. If anyone wanted to drop in to blow Vi's bulk apart it would be easy.

He strolled on, still mulling over the security problem when his uneasy thoughts were interrupted by the sound of a motor mower as Roberto broke cover from a patch of brambles. He slowed down and switched off the engine.

'Taking a stroll?'

I'm not climbing Mount Kilimanjaro, he thought irritably.

Sean nodded.

'How do you like your new job?'

'It's OK.'

'Vi's quite a character, don't you think?'

He nodded again.

Roberto gazed at Sean as if he was a mild but irritating joke.

'So you look after her.'

'That's what she hired me for.'

'And when Mr Fred comes home – will you be looking after him too?'

'I hope so.'

Roberto was short but strongly built and held considerable authority. He had obviously been a family retainer for a long time. 'She's upset, and here you are, wandering about the grounds. I thought you'd be sitting outside Mrs Cole's door like a guard dog.'

'I don't think she'd like that.'

'No?'

'I'm just having a look round to see how secure the place is.'

Roberto laughed derisively. 'Most of the fencing is down. So what do you think of that, Mr Minder?'

'Not a lot.'

'Maybe Maria and I won't have a job much longer.'

'Why?'

'Guys like you attract violence.'

'Without guys like me, you'd get a lot more.'

'Who's threatening Vi?'

'I'm not sure.'

'Is that all you're going to tell me?' Roberto looked indignant, as if they were both on the same level and would naturally exchange confidences.

'It's all I *can* tell you.'

'My wife and I have been with the family a long time. I need to know we're safe.'

'I'm afraid I can't give you any such assurances.' Sean was beginning to enjoy himself as Roberto became increasingly agitated.

'What about the black sheep?'

'Who?'

'Black sheep Eric.'

'What about him?'

'He's a threat.'

'Tell me more.'

'You an ex-copper then?'

The shock hit Sean like a physical blow. Did Roberto know something, or had he betrayed himself in some way? He racked his brains, hoping he didn't look as stunned as he felt.

Roberto's smile broadened, pleased to have scored. 'Most of you security guys have been in the police.'

Sean felt relieved at the understandable assumption. 'I've been in Cape Town, earning a bob or two but not as a copper.' He laughed too glibly. 'Wish I had. At least I'd have been better paid.'

There was a long and uncomfortable silence.

'You been a minder before?'

'Of course.'

'Where are your other clients? In their early graves?'

'They're all alive and well, pillars of urban society as far as I know.'

'The country used to be a healthy place,' said Roberto, starting up his mower.

'I'll try to keep it that way.'

*

Sean sat on a tree stump by the lake. The sky was dull and overcast and the water dark and still, choked with rotting weed and algae. He threw a stone which settled on the thick and scummy surface before dropping through to the depths. A couple of dragonflies skimmed the surface, carefully avoiding a toad, submerged except for a watchful head.

Sean hurled a stick into the morass and watched it float and then settle. For a moment, he thought he saw Abbie's face reflected in the scummy water, her eyes accusing. He got up hurriedly and almost ran back to the flat.

Once inside, he relaxed and poured out a whisky and tried to compose himself. Roberto was only trying to wind him up. He had been with the Coles a long time and was afraid his position would be usurped. There was no problem. As to Danny, he had surfaced again. For a moment, Sean couldn't work out what he was most afraid of – Roberto's scorn or Danny's sudden appearances.

Don't panic, said Kieron. Breathe slowly. Be vigilant.

He woke next morning with a headache, the result of continuous nightmares during which Abbie, Rik and Mary had stood on the lawn outside his bedroom window, gazing up at him beseechingly. Several times he had woken sweating, trying to force them out of his head, but had failed to do so. He had gone to the window, pulled the curtains aside and stared down at the empty grass.

Towards dawn his dead family became so real that Sean knew he could reach out and touch and feel them. He could hear their voices, smell Abbie's perfume, see Mary's tooth brace and the mud on Rik's knees after rugby.

He got up and made coffee, took some Disprin and gazed at himself in the mirror. He had never looked so drained. Then he reminded himself that it was Sean who had never looked so drained.

'You look washed out.' Vi was sitting beside him in the front passenger seat, magnificent in a lime green suit with a white lace blouse. The sun had broken through and the Three Tenors were back on the deck. They were going for a shopping expedition, one of Vi's favourite excursions. All was right with the world. For a while.

'I had a bit of a sleepless night.'

'What was the problem?'

'I was worrying if I was looking after you properly.'

'Why do you say that?' Vi sounded slightly alarmed at his lack of confidence and he wished he hadn't expressed himself so badly. Nevertheless, he ploughed on.

'The fencing round the garden is practically non-existent. Anyone could easily get in.'

'You been talking to Roberto?'

'And checking it out for myself. It's wide open.'

'We're not Fortress Sunningdale.'

'You may have to be if you want a professional job done.'

'And that's why you had a sleepless night?'

'We should revise the security arrangements. Get up a proper fence and an alarm system.'

'You're going to sleep with me? Is that what you want? Follow me everywhere – even when I take a leak?' She laughed raucously and Sean suddenly realised how much he had grown to like Vi .

'I don't think you're taking this seriously enough,' he reproved.

'You don't? Listen to me, Sean, I've taken to you. You're honest and you don't faff around. But I never asked for twenty-four hour protection and the sooner you realise that the better.'

'Suppose I think you need it?'

'I'm not leading my life banged up, and neither will Fred. I wanted a minder who was going to keep an eye on us at a difficult time, that's all. So listen to me, Sean. If you don't want us to fall out, do the job I hired you for, not the one Roberto's asking for.'

'He's shit scared. If anyone decided to have a go, he and Maria would be at risk too.'

Vi was glowering at him and Sean wondered if he had finally gone too far. Nevertheless he decided to push on, to convince her how rigorous he had to be.

57

'I've got ten days. Are you prepared to spend money on the fence, some alarms and a surveillance system? It'll be a good investment.'

'How much?'

'Maybe ten grand.'

'That's a lot.'

'You don't think it's worth it? Look – there's a lot of interest in the business. You told me that yourself.'

She frowned and turned up the Three Tenors until they were deafening. Then Vi turned them off.

'Fuck you,' she said.

'What does that mean?'

'I don't usually give in to anyone.'

Sean felt like saying 'Not even to Fred?', but he knew better than that. 'I need to protect you both.'

'It's a bad time to be looking good,' she said reluctantly. 'Fred reckons the Grim Reaper's gone hyper-active. So go ahead, but watch the cost. There's been so many of us gone down I reckon you might get a discount on the job.' She laughed but it seemed automatic, a humourless reaction.

Sean realised Vi had been afraid for a long time. Was that behind her afternoon drinking?

'While you're about it, you can't protect me from my Fred's blind devotion to his right little tosser of a son, can you?'

'Sorry?'

'It's true, you know.'

'What is?'

'I *have* taken to you.'

7

Sean spent the next ten days ordering and supervising the erection of a three metre high security fence, a CCTV system, as well as a series of alarms. Fortunately, the company he employed seemed to show little interest in the purpose of the installation, Roberto appeared to be more reassured and even Vi seemed impressed despite token complaints. 'We'll be prisoners,' she grumbled.

Would it make that much of a difference, wondered Sean. Vi was something of a recluse anyway, seeing no one and as far as he could tell receiving very few telephone calls. He had been very surprised. How could she be so isolated and still run the business? Were she and Fred merely titular heads, holding the purse strings and nothing more?

These and other questions nagged at Sean as he continued to work with the security company, only breaking off in the afternoons to take Vi out in the Mercedes, now carefully avoiding asking too many questions.

He drove her to Guildford, where they processed slowly along the river bank, to Hampton Court and Kingston, to Shere and Godalming, to Abinger and Dorking, usually ending up in a tea shop, an endless succession of Copper Kettles where a determined hunt for doughnuts was surprisingly often met with disappointment. Scones and strawberry jam, cakes and tarts, meringues and sponge fingers – but no doughnuts. In the end, they began to visit bakeries who brought out selections that Vi would review disparagingly. 'Not enough jam', 'not enough in the middle', 'not enough anywhere' were amongst her standard complaints.

They often returned to the café at Runnymede and the gliding swans where, despite the dearth of doughnuts, Vi seemed most relaxed.

Gradually, Sean had the impression that she was in a state of self-imposed exile until Fred's release. More worryingly, although he was sure they were no longer followed, he could see her occasionally tensing up, checking the back window of the Mercedes, uneasy but silent.

He was equally sure that at the end of the drive Vi would go up to her sitting room and get drunk. But her confidences were few and far between now and they would often spend their excursions in silence with only desultory conversation over tea. Despite this, Sean still felt a closeness to her, as if he had known Vi for a long time and consequently there was no need to talk.

A few days before Fred's release, she asked Sean to drive her to Newlands Corner, a 'beauty spot' near Dorking that overlooked a large valley. The mid-week car-park was empty and for a while Vi sat in the back of the Mercedes in silence.

Then she said, 'I see the fence is up and running.'

'It may be up,' he acknowledged, 'but the cameras aren't ready.' Sean paused. 'I wonder what your neighbours think?'

'I don't know them, dear – and I wouldn't give a toss anyway. Fred and I don't socialise much these days. We like to keep ourselves to ourselves. We've had a lot of heartbreak.' She sounded depressed and Sean waited hopefully. 'Of course, the business runs itself and I can trust the staff.' She paused. 'Pity I can't trust my Fred.'

'Trust him?'

'He'd do anything for that little prick Eric.'

'Even damage the business?' Sean risked the assertive remark.

Vi didn't reply for a while. Then she said, 'Fred thinks I've treated Eric wrong, but I know different. Fred and I, we've never had a ruck before.' She gazed reflectively at a shack of a café on the other side of the road. 'See that caff? Fred and I used to run out here when we had the bike.'

'Bikers, were you?'

'Lot of leather.' She laughed. 'Always been close, Fred and I. Never needed anybody else till Eric came along.'

'He was the oldest?'

'By two years. Then my Andy turned up. Right out of the blue when I'd miscarried three bloody times and the fucking quacks told me I'd never have any kids.'

Sean's mind raced. What was she saying? That she hadn't given birth to Eric? That he wasn't her son?

'Adopted, is he?'

'Who?'

60

'Eric.'

'Sort of. He was everything to me, my Andy,' she said, changing the subject abruptly. 'I found him, see?'

'You found Eric?'

'Andy.' Vi was impatient. 'I found him dead, didn't I?'

'I'm sorry.'

'I know Eric turned him on. From then on, we didn't speak. He never came to the house again.'

'But his father sees him?'

'Fred's a soft touch, isn't he?'

The café reeked of sour milk and leather. The windows were steamed up and old-fashioned Dunlop girlie calendars hung on the dirty white walls. Sean asked for strong, sweet tea and then made a major discovery. They sold doughnuts. He ordered a generous supply and Vi voted them not just good but 'fucking marvellous'.

'Jam in the centre,' she said. 'And plenty of it.' She gave him an affectionate grin. 'We've had some times, haven't we?'

'As long as you don't think I'm just waiting to top you.'

'After me spending a fortune on that fence? I don't think so. Fred's going to get the shock of his life when he sees what you've been up to.'

'He's not going to be pleased?'

'Not with the bill.' Vi wiped the jam from her lips and gazed round the greasy spoon café. 'Nice and cosy here, isn't it, Sean? Fred's homecoming isn't going to be easy. What with Eric and you.'

'Me?'

'Well, Fred doesn't know the extent. Get me?'

Sean said he did.

Vi slowly got to her feet and then sank back. 'You'll have to give me a hand up.'

For a moment she looked helpless and Sean was possessed by such a strong rush of affection that he was startled. It was the first time he had felt anything like this since the accident.

He grabbed Vi's hand.

'We're an item, you and me.'

'Sure you're OK?'

'Why?' She was immediately suspicious and Sean realised he had broken the spell.

'Thought you might be getting a bit down.'

Vi sighed. 'I've got a lot of responsibility,' she said. 'Just when I thought Fred and I might go out to grass. Now I can't bloody trust him, can I?'

8

Kenshall Open Prison was composed of chalet-like buildings set in a central park of mown lawns and an administration building that had once been a country mansion. The estate was enclosed with a high wall, but there was no sign of any barbed wire.

'Doesn't look much like a prison.' Sean stated the obvious.

'Used to be a nut house,' said Vi. 'Now it's for white collar fraud, petty crime, or veterans like Fred. They hope the old bastard will do a bit of rehab at knocking seventy. But he just plays along with the game.'

'What game?' asked Sean.

'Education, bridge, canasta and keep fit.' Vi laughed scornfully. 'Everything Fred loves to hate. He's even done Tai Chi and been to a meditation class. I reckon he has a kip.' She paused and then muttered, 'Of course that's what Eric does all the frigging time.'

'What?'

'Plays games, doesn't he?'

Sean checked in with security and then continued up the tree-lined drive, drawing up at the main building with a feeling of disappointment as he saw the figure waiting outside.

Who was this dumpy, gnome-like man with the skinny body? Holding a cheap suitcase, Fred Cole looked more like a commuter waiting for the wife to pick him up at the station than a gangland boss.

'All right, girl?' he asked as he opened the back door and Sean realised that all his personality was to do with his voice, which was rich and deep and slightly belligerent. Getting in the back of the Mercedes, he gave Vi a brush of a kiss. 'I could murder a gin and tonic. Let's stop at the Lily. Who's this then? Your toyboy?'

'Yours too,' Vi reminded him. In the mirror, Sean thought she looked particularly vulnerable and not her usual assertive self.

'Just think of me as a particularly protective chauffeur,' said Sean.

'Plenty to say for himself, hasn't he?'

'What did you want?' complained Vi. 'A yes man?'

'Would have helped. Thank God I'm out in the fresh air. One more day in there and I'd have killed the prick I was banged up with.' Fred leant back against the leather seat and closed his eyes. 'Freedom,' he muttered, 'is a Mercedes. Freedom is a wide-screen telly. Freedom is a large gin. Freedom is a game of pool. Freedom is the wife's arse.'

'I was wondering if I'd get a mention.'

'Put your foot down, Sean, or whatever your bleedin' name is. Get us down the boozer.'

'You're not getting pissed,' said Vi.

'Just half pissed then.'

'You can do that at home.'

'She's a nagging old cow. Don't listen to a fucking word she says. Get us down the Lily – like I said.'

'You don't want our Sean nicked for speeding.' Vi pulled a thermos out of the glove compartment and handed it to Fred.

'What's in this? Fucking cocoa?'

'It'll keep you going till we get down the Lily.'

He planted a wet kiss on the back of Vi's neck and chuckled in delight. 'Ice cold G and T. Nice and long. That's why I love my Vi, Sean. She's a regular marvel.'

She's going to have to be, thought Sean.

The Lily of the Valley belied its name; a solid red-brick pub that was more like a Victorian public library, squatting in the High Street with a large but empty car-park.

Sean glanced at his watch. Just on eleven. He wondered how long Fred and Vi were going to be drinking at the Lily and what sort of condition they'd be in when they came out. The sun had disappeared and the sky was a steely grey.

'Care to join us?' asked Fred. The request was more like a challenge.

'I'll just check the place out and then I'll come back and sit in the car. Don't want to get breathalysed, do I?'

'Sanctimonious bastard, aren't you? What are you expecting then? Gunfight at the OK corral?'

Fred and Vi got out of the Mercedes slowly and stiffly and Sean followed them across the car-park. They were holding hands and despite Fred's gnomic appearance and Vi's bulk, the Coles had a certain dignity.

They were leaning into each other, sheltering against a chilly wind when Sean overtook them, opening the door of the pub, smelling a warm staleness composed of flat beer, fags and room spray.

The ceiling was brown with nicotine and the floral furnishings merged into dark woodwork. The place was empty and there was no sign of anyone behind the bar.

Sean rang a small silver bell.

'Don't be impatient, dear,' advised Vi.

'Sure they're open?'

'Of course they're open. The Lily's always open for Fred Cole.'

As if in direct response to the name, a man with a heavily lined face and rather affected goatee beard appeared. He had a fag in the centre of his grey lips and his sleeves were rolled up to reveal pallid arms where white hair grew like coarse thatch.

'I thought you'd drop by, Fred. First day out, isn't it?'

'Don't tell the world.'

'The world hasn't showed up yet. What is it? Usual for you and the missus – '

'It's the usual.' Fred sighed and looked around him. 'I've dreamt about this place every day for two fucking years. The Lily. I've come home.' His voice cracked slightly. 'Call me an old fool but – '

'You're an old fool,' said Vi.

'I've longed for my old Lily for a long time – like a fucking eternity.'

Vi burst into 'The Lily of Laguna' in a rich, powerful contralto and for a few seconds the barman joined in with a reedy tenor. Fred grabbed Sean and planted a kiss on his forehead. 'Meet my chauffeur,' he said. 'He's going to watch out for me and Vi.'

Sean grinned. 'I'll go and wait in the car.'

'You're a good boy and I'll bring you back a packet of crisps,' promised Vi.

Sean sat in the Mercedes as the car-park gradually filled up with expensive coupés, rather as if a society wedding was taking place, with at least a couple of Rolls Royces, half a dozen Bentleys and a clutch of Mercedes.

Suddenly he realised that Fred and Vi had not just stopped off for a quiet drink in their empty mid-morning local. Instead, they were waiting to be fêted by the South London underworld, sure that the grapevine would do the same job as invitation cards might have done in different circles.

Sean watched the astrakhan coats and narrow pin-stripe suits arrive. The men were in the majority, but there were a few elderly women in sleek fur coats and most were in their sixties, some older. He got the impression they were wary, and many of them had chauffeurs, dressed in similar style to Sean.

When the car-park was full other vehicles began to pull up on the street, parking on double yellow lines and opposite driveways with 'No Parking' signs. There was a quiet, affluent arrogance to them. Sean had never seen anything like this before, not in this life or in his previous incarnation. Worlds within worlds, he thought.

Some of the chauffeurs gathered round the cars talking, while others sat in the limousines, listening to the radio or a tape. Deciding that another rendition from the Three Tenors might bring on a seizure, Sean closed his eyes.

But he was not to sleep for long.

'New kid on the block?'

'Eh?'

Sean woke to see a short, plump, white-haired man in a beautifully pressed uniform with a cap. His skin tone was pink and he was in his late fifties.

'The name's Rice. Sam Rice.'

'Sean Pollard.'

They shook hands awkwardly through the window.

'Vi's bloke.'

'I wouldn't say that.'

'She's never had a driver before.'

'Fred lost his licence.'

'It's not all he's going to lose if he's not careful.'

'What do you mean by that?'

'Lot of good men going down. It's what they call the drop list. My guv'nor's shitting himself.'

'Who is he?'

'Anthony Groves.'

'Oh yes?'

'You're wet behind the ears, you are. Don't you know him?'

'I've been abroad.'

'They say that's why Vi got you. No Brit connections. But what she forgets is they're international.'

'I don't get you.' Sean tried friendly ignorance. It seemed to work.

'They're powerful. If they want the business they'll take it.'

'What about Eric then?'

'Fucking nancy boy. Never had any time for that scheming little bastard. Disgrace to the name of Cole.'

'So it's true. He does drugs.'

'He does them big. But he'll get his come-uppance. They'll want the Gatwick ring just as much as they want the Cole business. Stands to reason, doesn't it? But you're not just a chauffeur, are you? You're her minder. That's what it's coming to nowadays.'

'What about you, Sam? Going in for a bit of target practice, are you?'

'Wouldn't have it in me.'

'Is your job on the line then?'

'No chance. Mr Groves doesn't penny-pinch like Vi. His minder's in the boozer with him now.' Rice was indignant.

'When did Midas start muscling in?'

'It seemed to happen overnight. I've been told it's the super-market culture. There won't be any small businesses left soon. You mark my words. No more corner shops. Just wall-to-wall Midas.'

'Can't someone do something?'

'No chance.' Sam Rice seemed to relish being a prophet of doom. 'This is the end of the good old-fashioned family business.'

*

To Sean's surprise neither of the Coles were drunk when they returned to the Mercedes, although Fred's prison pallor had been replaced by a pinkish tinge, and Vi was wheezing slightly.

'You're leaving the party early, aren't you?'

'We want to give them a chance to slag us off.'

Fred tried to relight a damp cigar. 'Nice to know we're still nice to know.'

'They were all there,' said Vi. She turned to Fred and kissed him on his withered cheek. 'Everyone we was dragged up with.'

As Sean drove out of the pub car-park, Fred yawned. 'I reckon I still got respect. That's what the older generation do for you. Our generation. It's the younger ones who've lost out.'

'Come on, Fred.' Vi wasn't going to let him get away with that. 'They just don't run as deep, that's all. Don't have our experience.'

She fell silent, staring ahead, and when she spoke it was as if Sean wasn't there and he realised, with considerable satisfaction, that he had passed the ultimate test. The good and faithful servant had become invisible.

'So what are we going to do about Eric?'

'Eh?'

'You heard. He was the buzz word in the Lily, wasn't he? You've got to make up your mind.'

'I don't want the business going outside the family. You know that. Not with fucking Midas like an on heat Rottweiler.'

'Eric's not family. I did you a favour, Fred. I brought him up. Wasn't that enough? Don't let him take over the whole bleedin' lot.'

'Better than Midas.'

'He's not going to stop 'em, is he?'

'We need to talk about this between ourselves, Vi.'

The good and faithful servant had lost out.

'Blimey,' said Fred. 'What have you turned the place into, Vi? Looks like a bunker.'

'It's a welcome home present,' said Vi. 'Sean's idea.'

'How much has this lot set us back?'

'A few grand. It'll be worth it, Fred.'

He gazed up at the wire and cameras in disbelief. 'This is fucking ridiculous.'

'You were the one who was on about Midas. We need the protection. Life's changed.'

'You've gone well over the top, girl.' He turned to Sean. 'You conned her into this lot then?'

'I'm just doing my job.'

'With a lot of commission?'

Sean pointed a remote controller at the gates, punched in a code and they opened silently.

'Fucking Fort Knox, isn't it?'

As the Coles got out of the Mercedes, Fred complained, 'I'm going to be a right laughing stock. What's got into you, Vi? You lost your marbles?'

For a moment they both looked old and indecisive.

Then Fred took her hand. As they walked towards the front door Sean was reminded of the shoe advertisement where two children set off along a winding sunlit road.

'Where the hell's Maria?' Fred grumbled. 'We got to crack a code to get in, have we? Didn't you tell her what time we was coming home?'

'Of course I did.'

'Then where the hell *is* she?' He kept glancing about him uneasily, as if Maria was artfully concealed somewhere.

Vi turned to Sean who was a few paces behind them, holding Fred's suitcase. 'I've gone and left my handbag in the car. Be a love and nip back and get it for me.'

Sean put the suitcase down on the bottom step and hurried back to the Mercedes.

Grabbing her bag, he was just straightening up when he heard Vi say, 'Wait a minute, Fred. This door's open after all.'

'What am I going to do then? Carry you over the threshold like the young bride you was?'

'I'm a heavyweight now.'

'I can still get my arms round you, girl.'

'I wouldn't try. You'll only give yourself a hernia.'

9

The breeze that had been fanning the birch trees had dropped and a squirrel was squatting on the lawn, completely still as the spring sunlight broke through clouds, catching Fred and Vi in a golden glow. They were laughing, half turned towards each other as if he was really going to carry her across the threshold.

The flash was so bright that it hurt his eyes and the brilliant whiteness exploded with a dull thud. Vi and Fred were figures in a photographic negative, dim, burnt-out, silhouetted in the sunlight.

The interior of the house seemed to implode and the blast caught Sean, slamming his body hard against the Mercedes, knocking the wind out of him. Then he found himself bouncing off the car and rolling down the steeply sloping lawn, gasping for breath.

When Sean struggled to his feet again, he could see dense smoke rolling up in a dark cloud. Two wings of St Tropez were still standing, but the central section and part of the roof had collapsed, while red tongues of flame shot up in vivid contrast to the grey smoke.

Sean began to run over broken masonry and glass-strewn grass, leaping burning fragments, towards the gaping hole where the front door had once been.

The squirrel was lying across part of a blown-out window-frame, dead but unmarked, and he was reminded of Rik's untouched, empty features. Then Sean saw a dark trouser leg poking out of the debris and recognised Fred's expensive slip-on black shoe that was still highly polished, with only a little brick-dust on the toe cap. He bent over, choking in the smoke, putting only the slightest pressure on the ankle which suddenly detached itself.

The leg had been torn off at the knee, ending in bloodied pulp that was soaking Sean's hand.

He let go with a whimper and the calf rolled down the steps to land on the gravelled drive below, lying incongruously, surreal in dappled sunlight.

He glanced round as more masonry fell, narrowly missing him, and then saw Vi lying on her back, half on the scorched grass of the lawn, half on the gravel, her big blue eyes wide open. Although one arm was intact, the other was cut off at the elbow and the blackened stump was covered in dark blood.

Her lips were moving as Sean stumbled towards her. She was gazing up into the air, staring at the blue sky. 'Weather's getting better,' she said calmly. 'I can see a patch of blue.'

'Vi – '

'Bit of a bang. What was that?'

'Something happened,' Sean explained inadequately.

'I can't move.' Her chest heaved and she began to bleed from the mouth. She was smiling. 'What happened?'

'I don't – '

'Freak thunderstorm, was it? We've been having them this year. We'd better go and collect Fred. I wonder if he's wearing his mac. Can't be too careful, that's my policy. You can't be too careful. Funny thing, I got my asthma back. Makes me feel I can't breathe. Is that you, Sean?'

'I'm here, Vi.'

'I'm going to pick up Andy from school. Will you drive me?'

'Of course.'

'I'll just get a bit of a kip first. We won't be late, will we?'

'Course not.' He was kneeling down beside her now, holding her one remaining hand.

Vi's eyes were filming over and a rush of blood streamed from her mouth. 'Got a doughnut?' she asked. 'The right kind? With jam in the – ' Then she slipped away.

'Jesus!' Roberto's squat, powerful frame was made insubstantial by the strands of smoke as he knelt beside her. 'Sweet Jesus.'

Inside the partly demolished central section of the house Sean could hear a hissing sound as well as the regular fall of masonry. The flames had died back, engulfed by the heavy, choking black cloud.

'You were no fucking good.' Roberto began to weep.

71

Sean closed Vi's eyes. 'Why don't you phone for an ambulance?'

He paused, listening. There was no need for they could both hear the sirens, probably about half a mile away. Had someone alerted the rescue services, or had the sound of the explosion been enough?

'Where's your wife?' asked Sean.

'Down at the summerhouse.'

'What's she doing down there?'

'Cleaning.'

'On whose instructions?'

'Vi's.' Roberto kept staring at her corpse, unable to take his eyes off her face. Then his gaze shifted to the rubble around him. He shook his head, rapidly turning away from the black-trousered limb, no doubt pretending that he hadn't seen the obscene thing.

'Fred couldn't understand where Maria had gone,' admonished Sean. He had to apportion blame, even on the lowest level, to shield himself from the knowledge that he had utterly and completely failed to protect them. All his elaborate, if last minute, precautions had been for nothing.

The sirens were getting closer.

Roberto's face was contorted with fury as he took a couple of steps towards Sean and for a moment he thought he was going to strike him. Then he stared down at Vi again, the tears flooding his cheeks.

'Not her,' he whispered. 'Not our Vi.'

A police car swept into the drive, followed by three fire engines, a vehicle with a huge extending ladder and platform, a van marked 'Rescue' and the ambulance that neither Fred nor Vi were going to need.

Sean stood back, watching unbelievingly. He had failed. He had been an amateur after all. The job had been beyond him. Farringdon had overreached himself.

He gazed at the devastation, what remained of the flames doused by the snaking hose-pipes, the cloud of smoke billowing and then lessening. The Coles had been successfully targeted. He was only an outsider looking in.

*

For the next couple of hours Sean could only feel a degree of lessening but merciful detachment.

When the fire brigade had finally extinguished the flames and Vi's corpse as well as all the bits of Fred that could be found were taken away, Sean, Roberto and Maria were questioned by the police in considerable detail.

A large truck marked 'Incident Room' had been parked on the ruined lawn and the interviews were carried out in its bleak interior which smelt of body odour.

As far as he was concerned, however, Sean had the impression that the interrogation was perfunctory, that the officer was simply going through the motions, all too well aware of his true role.

Towards evening, his numbness disappeared and the trauma of Vi's death merged with the carnage on the M25. He had only been with her just over a fortnight but he now realised how important she had become to him.

As he sat alone in his untouched flat over the garage, listening to the sound of builders making the rest of St Tropez safe, his mobile rang.

'Mr Pollard?' The voice was tentative. 'This is Eric Cole. I've heard what's happened.' There was a long pause. 'I'm in Geneva but I'll be flying home tonight.'

'I failed them,' was all Sean could manage to say.

'I'm not apportioning blame. My mother never listened to anyone anyway.'

'She listened to me. She agreed to the security fencing and – '

Eric cut in. 'You understand that she and I were estranged?'

'She told me.'

'No doubt Vi also told you that I was amongst those who would like to see her dead.'

'She never said that.'

Eric didn't seem in the least reassured,nor did he seem in the least embarrassed. It was as if he had an obsessive urge to be as truthful as he could. Or maybe that's what Eric wanted him to think. 'Despite the fact that she spent a lifetime – my lifetime – rejecting me, I still loved her. Of course, Dad and I were inseparable.' His voice trailed away and returned, the words almost tumbling over each other. 'I'm not going to try and convince you.'

'You may have to convince the police.'

'I've been in Geneva for the last few days.'

Suppose you hired someone to do it for you, thought Sean.

'I'd like to meet and have a talk. My mother held certain prejudices about me. You should find out for yourself how wrong she was.'

Sean didn't reply.

'Don't *you* want to find out who did this?' Eric's voice broke and there was a long silence. Then he continued more hesitantly. 'My mother got pretty close to you in a fortnight, didn't she? We need – we could help each other. I'll be in touch.'

After he had hung up, Sean wondered how Eric Cole had got the number of his mobile. Perhaps he had just been very persistent. In Sean's experience, lonely people often were.

St Tropez wasn't made secure until much later that evening, when metal supports were placed against the walls and the blown-out section was shored up.

Sean came out to view the blackened ruin again while Roberto and Maria made tea for the large number of officials and workers still on the site. Roberto scowled at him as he wandered about the debris, making Sean feel so unwelcome that he was eventually driven back to the oppressive confines of the flat.

Eventually, after a good deal of whisky, he managed to sleep, but was wakened just after three by a soft, insistent tapping.

Staggering blearily out of bed he called out, 'Who is it?'

'Police.'

Sean opened the door to a young DI.

'Mr Pollard? Farringdon wants to see you. 11 a.m. Rottingdean. There's a small pond in the village high street. He'll be there.'

Sean went back to bed and dreamt of Vi sitting in the steamed-up biker café at Newlands Corner eating her doughnuts. She was about to call for more when the door was opened and a comic-strip bomb rolled over the floor towards her, ticking loudly. Then the bomb turned into a doughnut.

The doughnut went on ticking.

*

'You're sure you weren't followed?'

'I took the most circuitous possible route.'

'Let's walk then.'

They strolled towards the South Downs, leaving the village by a steep track until, slightly out of breath, they reached open downland. Satisfied they were completely alone, they sat on a wooden bench overlooking a distant sea. The morning had a mellow warmth and the sky was a light blue, broken up by fleecy clouds that looked as if they belonged in a child's picture book. Sean felt an unexpected sense of relief, as if he had put distance between him and the traumas that had dogged him.

'You're not meant to be an action hero,' Farringdon began. 'You won her confidence before she died. That was the point of it all. That's what's going to stick with Eric.'

'He called me.'

'That sticking's beginning then. The good and faithful servant with the shortest possible track record. A fortnight, wasn't it? And now Eric wants to talk.'

'He probably only wants to find out what I know. He struck me as being as lonely as Vi.'

'That's a beginning. Looks like we're on target.'

'So were Vi and Fred. Is this Midas?'

'Or someone who hopes we'll think it is.'

'I was questioned for a convincingly long time. The police did a good cover job.' Then Sean came to the issue that had really begun to worry him. 'Suppose Eric thinks *I* killed them?'

'He might do. There's another angle though. The grapevine claims Vi wanted Eric out and that could have upset Fred.'

'But they both died.'

'By mistake?' suggested Farringdon. 'Forensic took a look at what was left of the timing device. They can't be sure but they think the bomb might have gone off prematurely.'

'Where was it?'

'In a little closet. Just off to the right of the front door.'

'Vi kept her handbag in there. She was always losing it and told me she'd fixed on keeping it in the closet so she'd always know where to find it.'

'Let's go through the possibilities then,' said Farringdon. 'One, Eric Cole kills his parents because his mother might persuade his father to disinherit him. Two, Fred was in league with Eric to kill Vi. That seems a very unlikely scenario. Three, one of their associates planted the bomb. If that's the case, Eric could be at risk himself. Four, Midas moved in.'

'What about the two Italians?'

'Urgent business in the summerhouse?'

'You reckon they could have been implicated?'

'It's possible.'

'What do the police think?'

Farringdon didn't answer directly. 'Roberto and Maria have been with the Coles for a very long time.' He paused for a moment. 'Meeting Eric will give you a chance to mull over all the possibilities. What about your cover? Any problems?'

'I'm still Danny Boyd if I lose my grip; it's impossible to be Sean all the time. I even try to read what he might like – I try to eat what he might like – to watch the TV programmes he might – '

'That's the way you should be thinking.' Farringdon was soothingly comforting.

'When I'm reading in bed I long for Robert Harris's *Fatherland*. I was half-way through that when the M25 happened.'

'Isn't Sean up to Harris?'

'He reads Stephen King.'

'And whose fault is that?'

'Kieron's.'

Farringdon laughed.

'I long to phone Kieron – to make an urgent plea.'

'What's that?'

'Is there life after Stephen King?'

For the next few days, the police guarded what was left of St Tropez and the forensic team returned again and again.

Sean kept to his flat. Roberto and Maria still made tea for their many visitors, but they didn't come anywhere near him. As a result he was partly thankful – and partly resentful. Worst of all, however, the expected contact from Eric didn't materialise.

He had to find something to do – and fast. A diet of daytime television was threatening to make him apathetic and the whisky bottle was an ever-present temptation. He also realised he would make a better veterinary surgeon than a minder.

To keep these denigrating thoughts at bay, not to mention the thrusting darkness of recent memory, Sean decided to fill his time more productively.

Years ago, Danny Boyd had been trained in firearms, but as Sean Pollard had had little chance to practise he decided to walk over to some thick woods at the back of the house. If Eric phoned he would be able to get him on his mobile, so he might as well wait amongst the trees as sit alone in his flat.

As he pushed his way through the dense undergrowth, he wondered what kind of game Eric Cole was playing with him.

Sean finally found a clearing that smelt of dank moss and generations of dead leaves. Taking out the silenced automatic, he gazed down at the matt surface and steel barrel, suddenly distraught by its deadly efficiency.

To his own amazement, Sean sat down on a fallen log and began to weep for Abbie, Rik and Mary. The naïve idea of being born again to avoid Danny's grief now seemed utterly ludicrous, his new identity no more than a hollow shell. Then Sean realised he was also weeping for Vi.

After a while, still shaken by dry sobs, he slipped the safety catch off the automatic and stood up, firing into the ivy-hung branches of a dead oak with dull little thumps. As the soft wood fell apart a startled blackbird rose out of the foliage.

Last year, he had camped out with the children in a similarly dense wood not far from home, and for a terrible moment he thought he could see the bright green tent in the next clearing. Then Sean realised he was gazing at a bank of verdant moss.

Strapping the automatic back into position, he turned away, wondering what to do next. Vi and Fred's funeral was set for tomorrow and he had a sudden urge to drive to the café at Newlands Corner and buy half a dozen succulent doughnuts to throw into her grave. He could almost hear her voice crying out from beneath the loam: 'Plenty of jam, is there? In the right place? You know what I mean, Sean.'

Next morning, he drove a silently hostile Roberto and Maria to the gates of Aldershot Cemetery. When he had parked the

Mercedes, they separated, still intent on avoiding each other's company.

The congregation consisted of the Lily of the Valley crowd all over again, resplendent in their astrakhan coats and dark suits, this time with ties and white shirts, the women stylish in their black jackets and skirts, slightly old-fashioned with their hats and gloves. There was also a scattering of younger men wearing the baggy suits of the nineties with short hair or ponytails.

The rain had sheeted down half an hour ago and the laurel hedges that ran round the perimeter of the cemetery were gleaming while large puddles lay on the tarmac as the drizzle continued.

As Sean trod the rain-washed pavements with umbrella aloft, he noticed an elderly woman, also alone, shivering in the pale, damp sunlight that was just beginning to break through the clouds. She was tall and still elegant, although her long oval face was deeply lined and there were liver spots on her hands. Unlike most of the other women, she wasn't wearing a hat, and her strikingly thick and straight blonde hair flowed down to her shoulders. He supposed it was dyed, but its silky softness looked magnificent. Somehow there was an authority to her apartness, and Sean approached her largely out of curiosity.

'Would you like to share my umbrella?'

'That's kind of you.'

'The name's Pollard.'

'I'm Elizabeth Gerrard, an old friend of Vi's. We were at school together.' As he held the umbrella over her head she lit a cigarette.

'Were you close?'

'More so since I sold up my hairdressing salons and retired.'

She reminded him of a hitch-hiker, swapping a life story for a ride – or in this case an umbrella.

'I heard about you.'

'Who from?'

'The horse's mouth. What are you going to do next?'

'I don't know,' he replied hesitantly. 'I'm really hanging about, waiting to talk to Eric Cole. He said he'd ring me.'

Elizabeth didn't reply, and as they were nearing the chapel Sean decided to try and press her a little more.

'But he hasn't contacted me.'

'He wouldn't come to St Trop.'

'Was his relationship with his mother that bad?'

Elizabeth was silent. Then she said, 'I think you'd like to know I spoke to Vi the night before she died and she told me how much she liked and trusted you.'

'I let her down.'

'That's as may be, but Vi was very alone. She needed you. You came at the right time.'

There was a long silence between them as the rain intensified. Then Elizabeth seemed to make up her mind to say more.

'Eric didn't stand a chance.'

'Why?'

'He wasn't her child. Fred had plenty of one-night stands, but usually he was more careful.'

'Did Vi know?'

'She allowed them. Fred couldn't get enough of it. Of course Vi forgave him, but she couldn't forgive Eric. He was one of her blind spots.'

'She had others?'

'Let's concentrate on Eric. I did what I could but it seriously damaged him. He can't trust anyone in the business – or anyone outside it for that matter. Of course, Vi always blamed him for Andy's death.'

'Do you?'

'I was never sure.'

'What was Andrew like?'

'A chip off the old block.'

'Whose block?'

'His mum's. He was like her, determined to keep the business clean.'

'She told me about that.'

Elizabeth hesitated. 'Vi always adored Fred, despite his little escapades, and that's the kind of woman she was. Good at business and a nice old-fashioned mum at home.'

'Did you see much of Andrew?'

'Yes. He was a good boy.'

'And Eric?'

'Ambitious. Resentful. The two are a bad combination.'

'Can you tell me more about him?' Sean knew he must sound like an interrogator but the opportunity was too good to be missed.

'Vi gave him a hard time. It shows.'

'Can't you give me any more?' Too late, Sean could feel the hostility rising between them and decided to backtrack.

'I'm going into the chapel to get myself a seat – and I'd rather you didn't sit near me.'

'Have I offended you?'

'Not in the least. I just don't want to be compromised, that's all, and we've had our unofficial chat. Don't let's turn it into an alliance.'

Sean cursed himself. She had seemed to want to confide. Maybe she'd even been waiting to do so, and then she'd abruptly withdrawn. How had he frightened her off? Or could it be the proximity of someone else? He looked round at the faces of the mourners, but they were all strangers to him.

Then Sean began to wonder why Elizabeth, like Eric, had been bursting with confidences. Had they both been anxious to influence him as much as possible? Did they realise they could need him in the future? Sean had the impression he was rather like a repository, someone to fill with subjective impressions.

The rain was still falling as the Coles' funeral cortège arrived, drawn by two ponies with plumes and gold harness. The carriage was black with silver tracery, its roof strung with white carnations that spelt out 'Vi and Fred Cole. South London's Best Loved.' There were more flowers massed on the back step and the driver on the box wore a faultlessly cut suit. A large, bullish clean-shaven man with swept-back blond hair sat next to him, an artificial tan on his fleshy face.

No limousines followed the carriage. Swallowed up by the crowd, all Sean could hear was the sound of hooves, the rustling of a rising wind in the yew trees and the steady patter of rain.

10

As Eric Cole jumped athletically down from the box, the crowd fell back, making a semicircle round the cortège; the pall bearers stepped forward and began to remove the two coffins from the hearse.

As if on an unspoken command, the mourners turned towards the chapel, and caught up in the flurry Sean felt a surge of panic when the massed South London families surrounded him, not allowing him to break ranks.

A bell tolled, sonorous yet slightly cracked, and Sean's umbrella was in peril of being dashed up against an expensively clad shoulder. The chapel door reared up, cherubims and seraphims gazing at him through centuries of soot as he was propelled into a dim interior that smelt of candle grease and beeswax. The organ thundered Handel's Largo, and the stained glass angels had trumpets to their lips sounding Fred and Vi Cole's final lament.

Sean was handed a service sheet and ushered to a pew while a young priest walked up the nave, his eyes downcast, followed by an Afro-Caribbean choir singing 'Jesu, Joy of Man's Desiring'.

The Bible readings and appreciations came from a number of elderly men and women who had an aura to them, a certain kind of distinction, and Sean guessed that the plain-clothes detectives mingling with the crowd were quietly identifying them.

The choir sang the sacred songs with exquisite clarity and many of the congregation wept. Despite his unease, Sean felt deeply moved, remembering Vi by the river at Runnymede, and later walking hand-in-hand with Fred towards the Lily of the Valley.

Then, as the funeral service drew to a close, Eric Cole mounted the pulpit, gazing down at his parents' coffins on their trestles just below the altar steps. There was a long, tense silence before he spoke.

'As most of you will know, I'm the only surviving son of Fred and Vi Cole and I still can't accept they're dead. They were always too much alive for any of us to believe that. But although Fred and Vi may have departed this life they can never leave our memories.'

Without warning, Eric broke down, and once again Sean Pollard became Danny Boyd as the grief spread inside him.

'They were killed in a way that none of us will forget and can ever forgive. Their murderers may well be here now.' He allowed a longer silence to develop while the congregation gazed straight ahead. 'If anyone knows who killed my parents, please tell me. It goes without saying that I'm offering a substantial reward for the information. Naturally, Thames Valley CID will be mingling with you afterwards.'

The priest gazed up at the pulpit questioningly, as if Eric was bringing the church into disrepute.

'Since my brother's death I'd become estranged from my mother, and although I still saw a great deal of my father I rarely visited Vi. Of course I *heard* a lot about her. She was a big personality. She made her presence felt – as many of you will be aware.'

There was subdued, reflective laughter and the young priest gave a dutiful smile.

'I remember my brother Andrew saying that Mum was a one-off, that there was no one like her.' Eric had come down the pulpit steps as he was talking and was now standing between the two coffins, a hand on each. 'Maybe we could be friends again, now, Mum. Dad always used to say, "I've never stopped loving her." Well, I never stopped loving you, either.' Eric stood silently for a few seconds, and while he was doing so Sean wondered about his real mother. Could she be here too?

Sean gazed round the chapel and saw that most people were staring intently at Eric, including Elizabeth, her hostility unmistakable.

Then he turned back to the congregation. 'Make no mistake. I'll find out who killed them.'

As if trying to drown his words the organist loudly began to play 'Rock of Ages'.

*

82

The rain had lessened as the mourners stood round the open grave with heavy clay on their shoes, as if the raw earth was determined to make its presence felt and give each of those assembled a taste of mortality.

The young priest began to intone, 'We therefore commit their bodies to the ground; earth to earth, ashes to ashes, dust to dust, in sure and certain hope of the resurrection to eternal life through our – '

'Vi.' The voice was urgent and demanding. 'Vi!' Someone was pushing their way through the crowd, someone who was tall and striking and determined. 'Don't let her go yet. Not yet.'

Elizabeth stumbled towards the open grave, holding a single rose.

For a moment Eric looked as if he was going to stop her, but she brushed past him, flinging the rose into the grave. Then Elizabeth stood, head bowed, in the rain.

Without thinking, Sean moved towards her, his umbrella aloft, and in the end they both pulled her back from the slippery loam at the edge of the grave. What would have happened if Elizabeth had fallen? Would she have landed on top of the coffin? Would the crowd begin to laugh? Or cry? But she was safe now, half leaning on Sean's arm, the rain turning to drizzle as the young priest continued.

'Through our Lord, Jesus Christ, who shall change our – '

Sean took a tighter grip on Elizabeth's arm as he felt her begin to shake.

'I'm all right,' she whispered angrily, trying to push him away.

When the final prayer was over, Eric threw a little earth on top of the coffins, almost intentionally dislodging Elizabeth's rose.

Sean didn't know what to do. Should he try and speak to Eric as they walked back to the cars, or would it be better to leave him alone? But if he didn't take the initiative, he might never be contacted again.

As he hesitated the crowd began to move, swallowing up Elizabeth, and a voice from behind him said, 'I'd like a word – if you've got a moment, Mr Pollard.'

The young man's leather jacket and dark grey trousers were unmistakably CID casual wear.

'I've already spoken to your colleagues,' he began impatiently.

'I was just hoping you'd spare a little more time for me.'

'Where shall we go?' Sean was grudging now.

'How about the yew tree over there? Just in case the rain comes on again.'

'There was someone I wanted to see – '

'We won't be long.'

Realising that his chance of speaking to Eric Cole had been sabotaged, Sean followed the CID officer to the yew tree, childishly keeping his umbrella to himself.

'Never seen so many of the mob. Real send-off.'

Sean said nothing.

'So what about your future plans?'

'They're fluid.'

'Are you still going to be employed by the Cole family?'

'I've no idea. This is a funeral – not an employment agency.'

'And in the meantime you'll be staying on in your flat?'

'For the moment.'

'I've been talking to Roberto and Maria.'

'Yes?'

'They were wondering who your former employers were. So am I.'

'I've had this conversation with your colleagues. Several times.' He suddenly realised the CID officer was conspicuously interviewing him at a highly emotive time. He should be more grateful. 'I've just come back from South Africa. I was in security.'

'Why do you think Mrs Cole hired you?'

'Because I came from nowhere. She felt safer that way. I didn't have any strings attached.'

'And because you'd been abroad, she couldn't have you checked out.'

'I needed the job and I got on well with her. Are there any more questions?'

'I shall need to see you again. The point is – '

But he never got to the point.

*

84

'Mr Pollard?' asked Eric Cole. 'I wonder if we could have a word – if you've finished your chat, that is.'

'Have we?'

The CID officer moved reluctantly away. 'For the moment.'

When he had gone, Cole said, 'Place is crawling with them. I have this feeling he was trying to keep you away from me.'

'I was expecting you to ring me.'

'Oddly enough I had other things on my mind.'

There was a long pause.

'If you got close to my mother, she no doubt told you that I do drugs. Well, I don't. Like you didn't plant that bomb. Unfortunately, both statements are unsubstantiated so we need to find out a little more about each other. My mother was very discerning. So am I.'

'You think I know something you don't?'

'You must understand I'm taking over the business – the business that Mum didn't want me to get my sticky little hands on. Dad knew what the truth was but he could never get her to believe in me.'

Sean was surprised to see there were tears in Eric's eyes.

'You loved her.'

'I didn't stand a chance. She hated the sight of me – ever since I was born. But she treated you like a son. Is that right?'

'Aren't you getting all this out of proportion? I was only with her for a fortnight.'

'How was she?'

'Jumpy. Isolated.'

'I didn't wish that fucking bomb on her.'

'Neither did I. But we've only got each other's word for it and what does that mean? Fuck all.'

'We'll find out the truth together then.'

'What are you getting at?' Sean was determined to stay on an equal level with him and not let a master/servant relationship develop.

'I wondered why Vi trusted you right off. Mum didn't know the first thing about you.'

Before either of them had a chance to say any more, a man began to walk towards them, somewhere in his early twenties.

'You're going to be late, Eric.'

'We've got a small reception.'

'Where?' asked Sean.

'At the Lily.'

'That's ironic.'

'Why don't you come?'

'Close family only, isn't it?'

'Not at all.'

'Is Elizabeth going?'

'No chance.'

'She claims to be your mother's best friend.'

Eric turned and began to walk away between the headstones, followed by the young man, heading for the gate. 'I'll ring you.'

'When?'

'When I'm ready.'

11

Sean spent another two days sitting in the flat above the garage. His recent target practice now seemed ludicrous and a heady lethargy consumed him. He slept for hours, completely exhausted from doing nothing at all.

Outside his hibernation, the spring weather improved and fragile sunshine filtered the debris of the ruined building.

The previous night he had dreamt that he was the guardian of a great castle that had been sacked by local peasants. Royalty deposed, he wandered the ruins, finding a gleaming diadem buried in charcoal. Something was stuck to the base. As he woke, Sean knew that it was a burnt doughnut, fried to a crisp.

The shoring up of St Tropez had been strengthened and the right and left-hand wings had been checked and pronounced safe. Rebuilding, however, was not just dependent on the insurance company but on probate as well and clearly wasn't going to happen for some time.

Towards the evening of the second day, Sean's exhaustion seemed spent and he longed to talk to someone. After a great deal of procrastination, he decided to find Maria and try to break down some of the barriers between them. One thing was certain, he couldn't make the situation any worse.

Wandering outside, Sean saw her providentially bringing in some washing from a small courtyard at the back of the undamaged right wing, and praying that Roberto wouldn't suddenly appear he strolled over-casually across, having invented what he hoped was at least a reasonable excuse.

'Could I have a quick word?'

Maria was startled and predictably unfriendly. 'What do you want?'

'Just to say I shall probably be leaving soon. I thought I should tell you now rather than – ' He broke off. 'I'll be talking to Mr Eric before I go. Do you know where he lives?'

'By the river at Walton-on-Thames.'

He looked at her searchingly, surprised to find the conversation continuing, however haltingly. 'Pleasant spot?'

'I've never been.' Maria paused and then her curiosity got the better of her. 'What are you seeing him for?'

'I'm not sure.' He paused. 'What's going to happen to you and your husband?'

'We wait.'

'For Mr Eric?'

'Like you.'

Well, at least we've got something in common, Sean thought. 'Why don't you both hand in your notice?'

'Roberto doesn't want to do that.'

'Why not?'

'We've been around a long time.'

'Didn't you bring Mr Eric up?'

'Yes.'

'What was he like as a child?'

'A handful.' She smiled and looked fractionally more relaxed. Then he wondered if it was because she was pleased he had said he might be going away at last.

'How do you mean?'

'He loved to play games.'

'Sport?'

'That too.'

'Were there other kinds of games?'

'He liked to play practical jokes.'

'Mr Eric sounds a real barrel of fun. You must have got angry with him.'

'Not at all. I was fond of him.'

'Which is apparently more than his mother was.'

'I don't want to talk about that.'

'You enjoyed his jokes though? Did he make you laugh?'

'He could be amusing,' she admitted. 'But he was often cruel.'

'Surely not?'

'Once he sent his mother an invitation to her own funeral. Another time he sent me and Roberto on a wild-goose chase to find some relations that didn't exist in Swindon.'

'What joke did he play on his father?'

'He didn't.'

'Why not?' he persisted.

'Because he – ' She broke off abruptly, and Sean saw Roberto striding towards them.

'What were you talking to my wife about?'

'Just brightening up wash day.'

'You go now.'

'Consider me vanished in a puff of smoke.' Too late, Sean realised his lack of taste.

Roberto silently watched him. Then, almost as an afterthought, he said, without raising his voice, 'We will do what is for the best.'

'I'm sure you will,' replied Sean. 'You're free agents, aren't you?'

Eric phoned late the next afternoon and Sean tried not to sound overjoyed.

'So you'd still like to meet?'

'I'm getting tired of being kept hanging around.'

'I'm sorry. I've been very busy with the lawyers over my parents' estate. Why don't you come over tomorrow morning? I own Fish Pie Island in the Thames. It's not far. There's an old hotel called the Silver Moon which has been crumbling away for a long time.'

'You live in a hotel?'

'I live alongside it, in a house called the Annexe. Park in the car-park at the Merry Harriers just outside Walton and come across the footbridge. You really can't miss the hotel. The Annexe has a pool with a bit of roughly mown lawn, but the rest of the place is pure jungle.' He paused. 'You don't have any attachments, do you?'

'I never make friends that easily.'

'I'm a bit of a loner too.'

It was impossible for Sean to tell whether Eric was mocking him or not. 'You're on your own out there, are you?'

'Not quite,' he replied.

*

Sean was making a fry-up, the only dish that he and Danny both liked. As he added onions there was a knock on the door and he turned down the stove.

To his intense surprise Maria stood on the step, looking oddly unsettled and unsure of herself.

'We're leaving.' Her face was pale, the skin tightly stretched across her cheekbones.

'Leaving?' Sean felt the shock waves coursing through him. 'I thought you were waiting for Mr Eric's instructions.'

'We've changed our minds.'

'So where are you going?' He was still considerably unsettled. There was something strange about her manner, something deeply self-conscious.

'Back to Verona.'

'You said you – '

'So I've come to say goodbye – from both of us.'

Sean heard the sound of tyres on gravel and went to the window to see a Renault Espace had come to a halt outside.

'That'll be the taxi,' she said, looking flustered.

'What's the matter?'

'Nothing. I have to go. Mr Eric ordered it. I – we have to get our bags.'

'Wait a minute – '

She paused, her eyes fixed on him imploringly.

'What's going on?'

'I told you. We're going to the airport and the taxi has come.'

'Where's Roberto?'

'Waiting for me.'

Sean didn't know what to do. He was sure something was badly wrong.

'You said Mr Eric ordered the taxi?'

'Of course he did.' She was more than flustered now.

'Come on.' He grabbed her hand and she only half resisted as he pulled her into the small hallway. 'What the hell's going on? Why are you so afraid?'

Maria was shaking now and wringing her hands. 'We're going to Italy.' She repeated the litany mechanically. 'We're going back to Verona.'

'Who fixed it?'

'I don't know.'

'Where *are* you going? It's not Italy, is it? You've got to tell me what's going on. You know we don't have much time. Why are you so frightened?'

'Let me go. Roberto will be angry.'

'Please, Maria. What's happening?'

There was a thundering on the front door which Sean hurriedly locked.

'Maria! Are you in there?' Roberto bellowed.

'Let me go,' she whispered.

'Not till I sort this out.'

Sean shouted through the letterbox, 'I'm not letting Maria out until I've had some kind of explanation about what you're doing – and don't tell me you're going to Italy because I won't believe you.'

'I'll break my way in.'

'I don't think so. Tell me the truth.'

But there was no reply and then Sean heard Roberto pounding back on to the gravel.

'You're making a mistake.' Maria seemed slightly more composed now.

'I can protect you.'

'Please let me out.'

An insistent banging began on the door again and Sean wondered if Roberto was back on the other side. Maria half ran away from him and Sean grabbed her round the waist, but she didn't struggle.

'Is someone going to hurt you?'

'Of course they're not. Don't be a fool. You're making a silly mistake – '

Sean let her go but Maria made no move to reach the door. She seemed frozen, unable to make a decision.

Then a voice shouted, 'I'm an employee of Mr Cole's. He's paying the flight back to Italy for Roberto and Maria Their bags are packed and we don't have too much time to get to Gatwick. Mr Cole will be very upset if they miss their flight.'

'He's being generous to us,' said Maria. 'I'm nervous of flying. That's why I looked – afraid.'

Sean hesitated. Could he have been mistaken? Surely not. He recognised raw fear when he saw it.

'Have Mr Cole ring me. Get him to reassure me personally,' he shouted back.

'We haven't got time.'

'Then I'm afraid they'll miss their flight.'

'We don't know where he is.'

'Try Fish Pie Island.'

'We already have. There's no reply.'

'Go to hell,' Sean said, reaching for his mobile phone. 'I'm going to call the police.'

Then he remembered he had left the damn thing in the Mercedes.

'I'm dialling now,' he bluffed.

Sean gazed in gathering amazement at the door which was shuddering under a number of heavy blows. The woodwork splintered and it finally sprang open, kicked in by a powerfully built man who stood on the threshold in a balaclava mask, holding a small but powerful automatic. The events seemed more theatrical than threatening. What could be going on? Why wasn't he more afraid? He glanced across at Maria. Why did she look like an amateur actress who couldn't remember her lines, who couldn't help appearing unconvincing?

'Get your hands above your heads.' The command in itself seemed faintly ludicrous.

Sean did as he was told. His own automatic was still in the shoulder holster under his arm and he wondered why in God's name he hadn't got it out. Was it because it *was* like amateur dramatics, with everyone playing their parts rather badly? Playing? The word sounded an alarm. Who played games? Wasn't it Eric?

'Come with us, Maria.'

She began to walk slowly towards him.

'Arsehole.' The man in the balaclava crashed his fist into Sean's face and then kneed him in the balls. The blows didn't belong to the world of amateur dramatics.

Sean went down, unable to breathe, the agony engulfing him, lying on the carpet, the waves of pain surging through him as the man took Maria's arm and led her outside.

Slowly he forced himself back on to his knees, gasping, only seeing a red-black veil of pain. As it began to clear he dragged himself to his feet.

Limping painfully to the window he noticed the Espace was still standing in the drive but there was no sign of anyone around at all.

He swore, pushed his way through the wrecked front door which was hanging loosely on its hinges, and forced himself outside, head splitting, his genitals in spasm, reaching the drive, crunching on gravel, wondering where Maria and her captor had gone.

Sean sprinted towards the courtyard, but there was no one there and he waited, listening intently. Cautiously, he pushed open the back door, went inside and then heard voices outside as if he was in the coils of a nightmare, running a race he couldn't possibly win. Hurrying towards a window that over-looked the drive he saw Roberto and Maria in the back of the Espace while a man in a cheap jacket and baggy grey trousers and brogues was loading their suitcases.

The sign on the vehicle's roof read 'Luxury Taxis & Limousines'.

Sean reached the drive just as the man was getting back behind the wheel.

'Just a minute.' He knocked at the window which slid smoothly down.

'Yes, sir?' His voice was quite different from Sean's assailant.

'Who ordered this taxi?'

'Mr Cole.'

'And where are you taking your passengers?'

'Gatwick, sir. For a flight to Verona.'

'This guy – he broke down my door, assaulted me and tried to abduct this lady. He was armed and – '

'This man is disturbed,' interrupted Roberto. 'He was Mrs Cole's chauffeur but the bomb caused him to have a breakdown and he's discharged himself from hospital. Please take us to the airport. Mr Cole won't want us to miss our flight.'

Sean glanced at Maria who was staring expressionlessly ahead. What were they all doing? The black farce was deepening.

Turning to him Maria spoke woodenly. 'It's going to be wonderful to see our village again.'

Slowly, the Espace began to move forward. The driver was shaking his head. 'Right nutter,' he said.

Eric's telephone number wasn't listed and when Sean tried Enquiries he was told Cole was ex-directory. He began to think frenziedly. Should he go over to Fish Pie Island now? He felt in a state of total indecision and could only gaze at the shattered front door, trying to come to grips with the complexity of what had happened. It was as if he had been part of a well-rehearsed spoof. But the dull ache in his balls and the dried blood around his mouth spoke of something that was beyond acting.

Forcing himself to think more slowly Sean ran over everything that had happened. Of one thing he was absolutely certain – the Espace had not carried the taxi sign when it had first arrived.

Then he heard the sound of tyres on the gravel again.

A ramshackle builder's van came to a halt outside the window with the sign – 'J. Godfrey & Sons – We'll fix it fast – Whatever it is'.

Sean had the feeling that the world around him was becoming too much to cope with and that the only solution might be to go back to bed with a hot-water bottle and pull the duvet over his head. Instead, he hurried outside.

'Can I help you?' he asked like a brightly spoken automaton.

A large, overweight, elderly man levered himself out of the van. 'You got some damage?' He looked at the boarded-up front of St Tropez. 'Didn't realise it was that big. I was told all you needed was a new front door – not rebuilding completely.'

Sean gazed at him in bewilderment. 'How did you get here so fast?'

'You *are* Mr Pollard?'

'Yes. But they've only just gone. You couldn't have known – '

'Mrs Corsini sent for me.'

'She's in a taxi on her way to Gatwick. They left two or three minutes ago.'

'I got a call from her mobile.'

'I didn't know she had one. And anyway – you just couldn't have got here in such a short time. It's impossible. Totally – '

'Look – do you want this door fixed or not? I've got another one in the back.'

Sean followed him to the rear of the van and stared inside. 'It's identical,' he said in amazement.

'What did you expect? One that didn't match? I've always worked for Mrs Cole. Can't imagine who hated her and Fred that much, can you? I was their maintenance man and I saw to it that I had spares of most things. Very exacting, Mrs Cole was.'

'Have you got Eric Cole's telephone number?' asked Sean in desperation.

'I don't work for him.'

This is incredible, thought Sean. Could it all be some kind of huge practical joke? Like *Candid Camera*? Like one of the games Eric used to play? The whole scenario raced through his mind with Maria arriving in his room, apparently in fear for her life, the balaclava'd man insisting on her release, breaking down the door, attacking Sean and then completely disappearing from sight, while the Espace that had not been a taxi became a taxi, taking Maria and Roberto away to the airport.

Test? Abduction? Joke?

'Better show me the worst,' said the builder who might not be a builder.

'This way,' said Sean, the sweat standing out on his brow, his mouth so dry he could hardly speak.

'Bit of a mess.'

'Yes.' Sean felt that he was expected to apologise, as if he was somehow responsible. 'I'll leave you to it then,' he said instead.

'You going somewhere?'

'Just for a walk.'

'I wouldn't go too far.'

'Why not?'

'I might need you.'

'To help? To pay you?' Panic swept Sean.

'I'll bill the estate.'

'Good.'

'But I'd like to know where you're going. Just in case I need you.'

'I'll be outside.'

'Where?'

'Whiling away my time. Watching the sunset.'

'All right for some.'

'Do you always turn out so fast?' He was so confused now he couldn't work out the passage of time.

'I provided an immediate service for Mrs Cole and she always made it worth my while. I'm sure the estate will do the same.'

'All right for some.' Sean tried to grin.

'It wasn't all right for the Coles though, was it?'

When 'J. Godfrey' had replaced the front door and driven away all in the space of about half an hour, Sean leant against the wall of the house, gazing down at the lake, seeing the water glinting in the evening light. Suddenly he had never felt so terrified in either Sean's short span or Danny's longer life. He walked over the gravel to the stone balustrade and sat on it, watching the light go. Then he turned to the blasted outline of St Tropez, chunks of broken masonry and blackened beams piled under the ruined façade. The bomb had happened – that was real enough. He saw again Fred's severed foot. He reheard Vi's dying words. That was all real enough. So what was happening now? Why was he the victim of such devastating, impossible events? He closed his eyes and then opened them again.

Unbelievably, the Espace was sweeping up the drive. The vehicle no longer bore the taxi sign.

The shock was so great he found for a few moments he couldn't leave the balustrade. Then he slipped down and stood waiting.

Eric Cole was at the wheel and behind him, on the back seat, sat Roberto and Maria. Roberto was smiling broadly, but as the Espace came alongside him Sean saw that Maria's expression was blank.

As Sean walked up to them Eric got out and Roberto joined him, leaving Maria inside.

'You blew it,' said Eric quietly and contemptuously. 'Where was your mobile? Where was your gun? Where was your protection? No wonder you fucked up my parents.' He slapped

Sean round the face and then slapped him again. 'You're an idiot. What are you? A fucking idiot!'

Sean reeled back, his cheek stinging, totally humiliated. The game had been played and he had lost. To retaliate would be unjust. A betrayal.

12

'I want you to come over to Fish Pie Island tomorrow morning,' said Eric as if nothing had happened.

Sean gazed back at him incredulously.

'My mother thought a lot of you and I want to find out why.'

'What do you want to talk to me about?' Sean tried to be angry, but all he could feel was shame and failure.

'In a funny sort of way I've always been a mummy's boy. I want to find out who you are, Sean, who you really are.'

'Is the visit another of your pathetic little games?'

'It might be the *great* game. Isn't that what Baden-Powell said? "Life's a great game." Think positive, Sean.'

He realised that to be compliant would be a disaster. Even if Eric knew who he was, and he had no idea how he could have found that out, he had to react better than this.

'What happens if I just tell you to fuck off?'

Eric turned to Roberto, and as if at a signal Maria got out of the Espace. 'Thanks, everybody. Let's call it a wrap.'

He got back into the car and drove away, leaving the awkward trio on the darkening drive.

'Good joke,' said Roberto appreciatively.

'Can't you hear me laughing myself silly?'

Sean glanced at Maria, but she had turned away and was walking towards St Tropez. When is a joke not a joke, he wondered. When it's a bomb?

Sean was watching a game show. He was also drunk. Or at least he had already drunk a bottle of wine and was contemplating another.

'Don't ever put yourself off guard,' Kieron had said. 'However bad things are, keep off the booze.'

And here he was, already slightly pissed. He had not done this before, not even after the accident. But this evening Sean had convinced himself the wine would make him much more relaxed and he might even get a decent night's sleep. He had not had this for a long time, usually waking up several times before dawn, trying to ward off Danny. Now he had the chance to sleep so deeply – that he wouldn't wake up if there was an emergency. But what emergency could there be? Surely Eric's games were at an end?

Sean went into his plastic kitchen with its plastic breakfast bar and opened the second bottle of wine. Fortunately, the Mâcon was far from plastic.

The dull thuds were far away and could well have been caused by a hammer or any other kind of blunt instrument hitting a hard surface. Then they came again – reminding Sean of something he couldn't immediately remember. Outside, at the back of the house, a night wind rustled the trees in the dense woodland. Dense woodland? Of course, he had taken the silenced automatic out there for target practice and the sounds had been identical to those he had just heard. Sean staggered slightly, gripping the table top, his hand skidding along the slippery surface until he almost fell.

He pulled out his automatic, quietly opened the window and gazed out. The drive was empty. An aircraft droned overhead.

Sean ran lightly down the stairs and opened his new front door. Something stirred, sliding past him, and he started as the paper bag blew across the gravel.

He headed out past the shored-up building, keeping in the shadows, not wanting to be starkly outlined by the moon that rode the cloudy heavens, occasionally extinguished but soon reappearing.

Sean reached the courtyard and tried the door to the kitchen, above which Maria and Roberto had their flat. It opened immediately and in the pale moonlight he saw a flight of stairs leading up from behind the range. He stood at the bottom, listening intently, but the silence was dense and blanketing. Or was it? Wasn't that a sigh?

'Is everything all right?' he called.

The silence seemed to deepen.

Holding the automatic in both hands, Sean ran up the stairs, searching for a switch but taking a frustratingly long time finding one. Then he flooded a small, scruffy, disinfectant-smelling landing with tepid light, seeing flock wallpaper and a hideous Victorian hat-stand on which lay an incongruous deerstalker.

A door was uninvitingly half open.

Again, Sean heard the sigh, much fainter this time.

'Is everything all right?' he repeated, still holding the gun in both hands, edging forward and then pushing the door fully open.

The room was in pitch darkness. Sean fumbled for the switch and eventually found a cord.

Unlike the landing, the light was bright and hard and he blinked up at the bulb for a few seconds, not wanting to shift his gaze, gradually lowering the automatic. Then Sean forced himself to look down at the bed.

Roberto lay on his back with most of his face blown away. Beside him, Maria's head rested on his shoulder. There was a hole in her chest through which blood was still pumping and the sheets, the bed, even the walls were stained.

He stared down at her, again hearing that gentle sigh. Maria's eyes were tightly closed.

Whoever had shot them could still be around, thought Sean desperately. Then he wondered if he was gazing at stage blood or careful make-up. Was Eric hiding somewhere, waiting to spring out and accuse him again? He felt the stinging slap and the anger and the overwhelming sense of failure.

The sigh came again.

'Maria?'

Her lips twitched and she moved her head slightly as her eyes opened. She whispered something he couldn't understand.

'What is it? What are you saying?' He took her hand which was hot and dry.

'Mr Eric . . .'

'Did he do this?'

Her hand trembled in his.

'Did he do this?' he repeated. 'Did Mr Eric hurt you?'

This was no game. This was for real.

Maria's pulse was very faint, a mere fluttering like the wings of a trapped butterfly in the palm of his hand.

'Hang on. I'll get help.'

The wings stopped beating and he knew she was dead.

Sean got up and stood watching them. Then the police siren sounded at a distance and he knew he had been set up.

He saw a tissue in a half-open bedroom drawer and grabbed at it, scrubbing at Maria's wrist. Had he touched anything else? What about the light switches? The siren wailed closer.

Sean checked around him, and then calmed down. He would be all right. He *was* the police. After the initial arrest, there would be intervention. But then he suddenly realised his cover would be blown apart.

What would happen then? But Sean knew all too well. The investigation would be over, Danny would be waiting for him and the world of his grief would close in again. He *had* to be Sean.

He had to carry on.

Looking out of the window and beyond the courtyard he could see the wood where he had done his target practice. Below the sill was a flat roof from which he could jump on to the lawn, and providing he didn't break anything Sean thought he might have a slender chance of getting away.

Pulling open the window he struggled out, running to the edge of the roof, hesitating, and then jumping down as the squad car raced up the drive, scattering gravel.

The wood was as dense as ever, a thick tangle of ivy-covered trees and spiky, clinging undergrowth with a dusty, evergreen smell. Sean crouched under a canopy of dead, lichen-covered branches, trying to regain his breath.

But he knew he couldn't hide for long because this would be the first area for a police search. The disappearance of a chauffeur and the discovery of two bodies would be just as incriminating as being found standing over them with a recently fired automatic – the gun that he must get rid of as soon as he could.

Sean pushed on, gasping for breath, and the wood slowly thinned out until he was standing on the side of a narrow road that wound its way through exposed and gradually rising heath-land. There was no cover at all. Going back into the wood would be fatal, but to continue, a sentinel figure in a soon-to-break dawn, was ludicrous.

Sean felt as trapped as he had been in the house, and when he heard the sound of an approaching vehicle he desperately sought a ditch that wasn't there, hurling the automatic, covered with his fingerprints, into long grass.

The laundry van ground to a halt beside him, and Sean gazed back at the driver, wondering if he was going to ask for directions. Then he recognised him as 'J. Godfrey'.

'Mr Pollard?'

Sean hesitated and then said, 'Who wants him?'

'Mr Cole.'

'Eric Cole?'

'Get in the back.'

'What the hell for?'

'J. Godfrey' sighed patiently. 'If you don't the old bill's going to have us, isn't he? Why don't you just do what I say?'

Sean hesitated. 'So where are you going to take me?'

'To Mr Eric's house on Fish Pie Island. You'll be safe there.'

'I've left all my stuff in the flat.'

'I'll deal with that. Now get in and cover yourself up.'

Sean went round the back, opened the doors and closed them carefully behind him as the van began to move away. In the semi-darkness he slid his way into a heap of dirty laundry.

As he lay there, he thought about Maria and Roberto. Had Eric killed them? If he had, why hadn't he picked him off too? Or were other people involved? Like the Coles' maintenance man who was driving a laundry van and working for Eric, a role he had earlier denied.

They drove slowly on for about an hour until a grey dawn could just be seen through the back windows. Cautiously peering out, Sean saw that 'J. Godfrey' was taking B roads and keeping well within the speed limit.

He returned to his swathe of foul-smelling laundry and

covered himself up again, continuing to speculate with mounting apprehension.

The van eventually came to a halt and the doors were opened. It was still dark, but Sean could hear a roaring sound that he thought might be the sound of a weir on a river.

Eric Cole, dressed in T-shirt and jeans, was gazing down at him. 'I'm afraid I can't indulge your fantasies with dirty knickers any longer.' His eyes were slightly swollen. 'You've just got to repress these obsessions.'

'Who killed them?' Sean asked as he got out, his head splitting.

'Someone who likes to neaten up a job. Roberto always was an overbearing bastard, but Maria – she brought me up. I loved her.'

'J. Godfrey' was driving away, leaving them standing by a wooden footbridge. A battered and faded finger post read 'Fish Pie Island – Strictly Private'.

'Do you know what happened?' asked Sean.

'Roberto phoned me. He said he thought he'd seen someone in the garden, but by the time I arrived it was all over. They were dead.'

'You're wrong. Maria was still alive.'

Eric gazed at him incredulously. 'You're talking shit.'

'What time did you arrive at the house?'

'About three.'

'I was with her at just after three thirty. She was alive. Just. Maybe you didn't give a toss for her either?'

Eric seemed to lose control for the first time. 'I told you – she was dead. Fucking dead.'

'She mentioned your name. *Then* she died.'

'I could have made a mistake.'

'I reckon that evens us up then. On mistakes, I mean.'

Eric was silent and Sean thought he looked afraid.

'Why didn't Roberto ring *me*?' he demanded.

'Probably thought you were fucking useless, or more likely he suspected you might kill him.'

'How come you didn't wake me either? Or was it a set-up? Did you want me to get done for them? Because if I was, I'd be done for your parents too. Now that *would* be nice and neat.'

103

'I'm sorry. I didn't want to involve you. I was too gutted by what I'd seen.'

'So it wasn't another game.'

'Don't be a fool.'

'You wanted to set me up. You must have done. I was most likely to have slept right through it – until the old bill arrived, that is.'

Eric paused. 'I saw you come out of the flat.'

'So why didn't you warn me?'

'How was I to know whether you'd killed them or not?'

'So why rescue me?'

'I had a last minute change of heart.'

'Bollocks. You'd called the police.'

'Naturally.'

'And what would have happened if they'd arrested me?'

'If you'd allowed yourself to get done, then I wouldn't have wanted you here.'

'I told you – I could have slept through the whole damn thing.'

'You could have done. But you didn't, and later you used your initiative and did a runner. I like that. Now we can give you an alibi. Last night you were having a meal with me and a couple of mates. We'll vouch for you.'

'Why should I trust a word you say?'

'I can't think why you should – but you've got to take a decision, Sean. You've got to stand up and be counted.'

'The problem is I don't know who I should be counted for, or even why I'm here.'

'You need a shower and some sleep. I'll have to talk to the police and, later on, so will you.'

'And then? Do *I* get murdered in my nice snug little bed, just like Roberto and Maria?'

'I much prefer you alive.'

'Why?'

'I'm going to suss you out, aren't I?'

Sean was silent. Then he said, 'Tell me something.'

'What is it?' Eric was impatient now.

'Why do you *really* want me here?'

'Put it like this, Sean: neither of us trusts the other, but both of us have been pretty well tested and will be again. We're both suspects for two sets of brutal murders and so, in the end, aren't we better off together?'

'Why don't you come clean with me?'

'Why don't you?' Eric began to walk towards the footbridge. 'For the moment there's nothing else to say – except that I'll be going abroad again soon and I thought you might like to come along for the ride.'

'Where?'

'Sunny Spain. You look as if you could do with a bit of a break.'

Fish Pie Island was a wilderness and its abandoned hotel, the Silver Moon, with crumbling verandas and weather-stained clapboard, was dank and oppressive. Dusty foliage had grown through the floor of the veranda; ivy covered some of the windows, climbing up one side of the building and rising as high as the broken chimneys. The hotel was low and rambling, constructed to resemble a riverboat with twin cupolas as funnels, one of which had collapsed into the decayed roof. Next door was a bungalow that looked rather more habitable.

'I bought the place cheap as an investment and when the market's right I'm going to sell it again. The pool's over there.' Eric pointed to some weeping willows by the river bank.

A lawn like a hay field, freshly cut but almost completely brown, surrounded scarred concrete and Sean caught a flash of blue.

'There's a squash court that's still usable.'

'So you're alone here.'

'That's nothing new. I grew to appreciate glorious isolation with Mum, didn't I? Now I insist you get some sleep because, if you don't, you're not going to be any use to me. I want you fresh for this afternoon.'

'What for?'

'I thought we'd have a game of squash.'

'At a time like this?'

'We need to use up some aggression.'

'Against each other?'

Sean had a feeling of dread and remembered an older boy at school who, for no apparent reason he could recall, had demanded to fight Danny behind the cricket pavilion, a long way from the sanctuary of the school buildings and the possible intervention of authority. But when he had trailed out to meet him, the boy had not been there. Now it was as if his opponent had returned, having waited for him all these years.

The bungalow was stylishly furnished, with hessian wall hangings, wooden floors and sandalwood furniture. The rooms were light and spacious and the place smelt clean, aromatic. In the kitchen, to Sean's consternation, a flesh-coloured sculpture, made of some kind of ceramic, stood in a corner. The nude woman, complete with ginger pubic hair, stared with exquisitely raised eyebrows up at the ceiling.

'She's my live-in partner,' Eric explained. 'But she'll have to go. Maybe you'd like her up in *your* room.'

'Why do you want to get rid of her?'

'Don't be denigrating. She's already offended because I've just acquired a real-life, walking, talking replacement.'

'Do I get to meet her?'

'You might be better off with my plastic dildo. Her name's Delilah.'

Despite the certainty that he would lie awake attempting to explore Eric's labyrinth, Sean plunged into deep sleep and woke refreshed. He gazed round the sunlit bedroom he had hardly noticed earlier, but the subtle oatmeal décor, muted floral prints, wide-screen television set and pine cocktail cabinet brought him little comfort. There was a brooding atmosphere as if something was about to happen that he wasn't going to like.

Was Eric really grieving for the mother who had so totally rejected him? Did he really care about Maria? More to the point – had he killed them both? And why the hell did he want him to go to Spain?

'Mr Eric.' Maria's last words beat in his mind. 'Mr Eric.'

Sean got up and went to the en-suite shower whose powerful, noisy jet of water made him uneasy. Several times he turned it off and parted the curtain to listen, waiting to see if someone had come into the room.

The telephone rang, making him jump so badly that his heart pounded. Wrapped in a towel Sean hurried to answer it, only to hear the dialling tone, eventually realising the ringing was coming from an internal phone on the wall.

'Sleep well?' asked Eric.

'OK.' Sean glanced down at his watch. It was just after midday.

'How about a bite to eat and a little walk? Then we can have our game of squash.'

'I haven't played in a long time.'

'I'll go gently on you.'

'Why do you need to do this?' Sean was determined to back out. 'It's hardly the right time – '

'I told you. I want to get to know you. Squash is the *Reader's Digest* crash course in perception.'

'That's a stupid thing to say.'

'Is it?'

'I enjoy cooking.' Eric was more benign in the kitchen, but he looked emotionally drained. 'How are the curried prawns?'

'They're good.' Sean had been surprised to find that he was ravenously hungry, and he consumed the curry and a wide selection of side dishes with relish. There was no wine, but cold, sparkling mineral water. 'Have you seen the police?'

'Whilst you were in repose. I told them we'd had quite an evening, that you'd got dead drunk and were sleeping it off. They'll be back to see you this afternoon.'

'I'm surprised they were so pliable.'

'I was very persuasive.'

'I would have thought I was the prime suspect. First your parents, then Roberto and Maria. I'm the only one left alive in the house of death.'

'It does look bad, but you're very inexperienced. Even the bill know the Coles have enemies – like queuing up to have a poke.'

'Were Midas involved?'

Immediately Eric's sense of humour evaporated and Sean had the immense satisfaction of seeing him look agitated.

'Who told you about them?'

'Vi. Something about a bent monetary fund.'

'They wouldn't be interested in the business.'

'Why not?'

'It's not big enough.'

'Vi wouldn't agree.'

'Vi wouldn't know.'

They had reached an impasse and Sean didn't want to push any further. Not at the moment anyway.

'I suppose it's all over the media.'

'The *Evening Standard* will have the story in their later editions, but I took the trouble to record the television news for you.'

'How thoughtful.'

'Want to watch while we eat?'

'You think it'll sharpen my appetite?'

'And save on conversation.' As Eric switched on the TV set the shattered façade of St Tropez appeared on the screen. 'Did gangland killers revisit Sunningdale's bomb site? Roberto and Maria Corsini, long-serving domestic staff employed by bomb victims Violet and Frederick Cole, were shot dead last night. The blast-damaged mansion in Sunningdale has been cordoned off by police while more forensic examinations are carried out.

'Detective Inspector Toby Dyson, now heading up the enquiry, spoke to our reporter Nigel McKay.'

Dyson: 'There's little doubt that the killings of Frederick and Violet Cole and their domestic staff Roberto and Maria Corsini are linked. We're treating all four killings as part of a gangland vendetta and a number of men and women are helping us with our enquiries.'

McKay: 'Would you consider these deaths are an escalation of the South London gang killings that have been carried out over the last few months?'

Dyson: 'It's certainly possible.'

McKay: 'Do you have any idea who is behind them?'

Dyson: 'As I said, a number of men and women are already helping us with our enquiries.'

McKay: 'Do you know for sure that Frederick and Violet Cole were involved in criminal activities?'

Dyson: 'They were an old-established South London family who we believe were involved in serious crime.'

McKay: 'Do you think they might have been responsible for the other killings?'

Dyson: 'We think that's unlikely.'
McKay: 'Are we likely to see more violence?'
Dyson: 'It can't be ruled out.'
'This is Nigel McKay, News at One, Sunningdale.'

The unmarked car arrived half an hour later and contained three police officers, two of whom remained with Eric while the other, middle-aged and comfortable, took Sean upstairs. Before he began his questions, he checked the bedroom conscientiously.

'It's not bugged.'

'Better to double-check, sir.'

'I've already done that.'

'Another pair of eyes always helps.'

'You know who I am?'

'Of course. I'm here to see how things are going and report back to Mr Farringdon.'

Sean breathed a grateful sigh of relief. The contact was like being brought out of the cold into a warm room where he might meet sense and logic rather than a series of complicated games. Why *was* Eric clouding the picture to such an extent?

'Cole has asked me to travel to Spain with him, but I can only assume he wants to find out what I know – which doesn't amount to a lot.'

'He's going to be disappointed then?'

'I'm afraid so.'

'It seems a long way to go to suss you out.'

'That's what I thought.'

'What did he give as his purpose for travelling there?'

'He won't tell me. But his mother suspected he was involved in a drug-trafficking ring at Gatwick.'

'Is that why she disapproved of him so much?'

'It goes much deeper than disapproval. She also believed he turned on her younger son, Andrew. He died of a heroin overdose. Naturally he denies everything.'

'He would, wouldn't he?'

'All I know for sure is that Andrew was Vi's natural son and Eric is a product of one of Fred Cole's liaisons.'

'She didn't like that?'

'Vi always took it out on Eric, and while I was working for

her she was at loggerheads with Fred, who was planning to bring him into the business. Now I suspect he'll inherit the lot. Whatever the lot really is.'

'So Eric's your prime suspect.'

'Not necessarily. Other criminals could be involved, including Midas. Farringdon knows about them already.'

'Are there any other reasons why you think Cole wants you close to him?'

'Maybe because he thinks I killed his family. He could be lining me up for execution.'

'That's a cheerful thought.'

'I met this woman Elizabeth Gerrard at the Coles' funeral. Do you know anything about her?'

'I'll try to find out.'

'She was an old friend of Vi's –'

'What about her other associates? Can you name anyone else?'

'What associates? Vi seemed to work in isolation.'

'What about Roberto and Maria? Any idea why they were murdered?'

'Eric played games with them, to test out my efficiency.'

Sean began to explain what had happened, watching with some pleasure the sheer incredulity that was stealing over the officer's face.

'Unfortunately I fucked up.'

'This guy's really weird.'

'That's an understatement.'

'You could be well in the shit.'

'That's *not* an understatement.'

When the police officers left, Eric, dressed in a fawn tracksuit, suggested they take a look at the pool 'to give you more time to digest your lunch'. As he spoke, he glanced at Sean with a mocking patronage.

Sean had never liked squash, associating the game with mindless, male competition, the legal duel of the twentieth century with its brutal body contact. Then he realised it was Danny who had disliked the game, Danny who had sought to prevent his son playing, Danny who had the rooted prejudice.

Sean had to keep his mind open. Above all, he had to lose
Danny Boyd.

The pool was like a David Hockney print. The blue seemed flat,
painted-on water that was lifeless and unrippled. There were no
trees to shed leaves on the pristine surface and the paving
around its sides was immaculate.

'Order in the wilderness,' said Eric.

'Are you going to restore the garden?'

'If I manage to resolve a few problems, I'll have more of the
wilderness tamed. In fact, I just might do it myself.'

'Why do you want me on this little jaunt to Spain?'

'I haven't got time to explain now.'

'Not even a hint?'

'I don't think so. Now how about our squash?'

'You're quite a games fanatic, aren't you?'

'When I was a kid I thought games were safe havens, somewhere you could take shelter, and for some reason I've always
remembered a poem I read at school. Every word sticks in my
mind and strikes a chord. Want to hear it?'

'Feel free.'

> 'There's a breathless hush in the Close tonight,
> Ten to make and the match to win.
> A bumping pitch and a blinding light,
> An hour to play and the last man in.
> And it's not for the sake of a ribboned coat,
> Or the selfish hope of a season's fame,
> But his captain's hand on his shoulder smote,
> "Play up! Play up! And play the game."'

'The greater the game,' said Eric slowly, 'the lesser the pain.'
Sean looked away, realising he was being laughed at.

The match was all that Sean had feared, until his adrenalin fired
and he began to feel more resourceful, despite the baggy tracksuit he had been loaned by Eric which was proving a substantial

111

handicap. However many times Sean rolled up the sleeves they soon descended again, hanging over his wrists and getting in the way of his stroke. In the end, with the first game at 5:3 against him, Sean tore off his top and threw it into a corner.

'It's too fucking big,' he yelled at Eric who immediately stripped off his own trimmer version, revealing a gleaming white T-shirt below. He then took off his tracksuit trousers to show equally pristine white shorts.

Forced to stay with the baggy tracksuit bottoms that were already damp with sweat, Sean raged inwardly. Eric was like some spoilt child, ensuring his opponent was as uncomfortable as possible, typically a game within a game.

The battle intensified until Sean narrowly won the first game and edged into the lead in the second. Fuck you, he thought as they worked on their strategies. Fuck you. Then Eric called foul over a fault that Sean was sure was nothing of the kind.

'That's not obstruction. I wasn't between you and the ball.'

'You fucking were. If I'd raised my racket I'd have smacked it right up your arse.'

They were facing each other now, the sweat pouring down their faces.

'We'll play on. I'll take the point.'

'You won't.' Eric swung at him. Sean retaliated by kicking his legs away from under him and he landed on the concrete floor with a grunt, letting go of his racket which slid across the court into the opposite corner.

He got to his feet, fists clenched.

Sean turned away, but only to place his own racket against the wall. He had a feeling of liberation, of getting, at last, beyond the game.

At first they punched wildly, eventually settling down into a more considered strategy, trading blow for blow just as they had traded stroke for stroke. They made no sound except for the squeaking of the soles of their trainers on the squash court floor and the rasping of their breath, with an occasional gasp as a punch made contact.

Slowly, Sean knew he was weakening, seeming to lack Eric's

purpose, and when they clinched he hung on to him, snatching precious seconds of relief.

The second time they clinched, Eric seized him round the waist and they fell to the floor, no longer punching but rolling over and over until they hit the wall. They lay there, straining against each other, with Eric partly on top, pressing down on Sean.

Then he kissed him full on the mouth.

'For Christ's sake – '

Eric got off him, his hands brushing Sean's knees until he was standing above him, uneasily triumphant.

'Sorry about that.'

Sean was still deeply shocked at what had happened as he dragged himself to his feet. In fact he could hardly *believe* what had happened. Eric had kissed him and he had felt his tongue. Was that why he had been tested and selected, whatever the dangers to both of them? To Vi a son. To Eric a bit of rough trade, another task for the good and faithful servant.

'Boys will be boys?' The voice from the gallery was doubtful, and Sean started, craning his neck to see a tall woman dressed in a white suit, her oval face framed by dark hair.

How long had she been there, he wondered. And just what had she seen?

'Fighting over your squash match? I always thought it was a kids' game.' Her voice was the product of a girls' public school.

Had she seen the kiss, wondered Sean, his lungs still hammering.

'We were having a bit of fun, weren't we?' said Eric anxiously.

'Just delayed adolescence then?'

'Kate Bradman – Sean Pollard. He's my new driver.'

'Am I?'

'Hello, new driver.'

Sean gave her what he hoped might be a casual grin. Inside he felt as if he had been caught out.

'Have you finished?' she asked.

'Yes.'

'Finished fighting, I mean.'

113

Eric frowned.

Kate strode across the balcony towards the door. 'I need some fresh air,' she said.

They strolled uneasily out of the squash court and down to the wilderness pool.

'You two look as if you should cool off,' said Kate.

'Why don't you join us?' suggested Sean, still wanting to keep the initiative. What the hell had Eric meant about him being his new driver?

There was a short, rather tense pause, as if they both thought he had stepped out of line, and he felt a flash of anger.

'Why not?' said Eric.

'I don't have a costume,' said Kate warily.

'Let's skinny dip.' Eric pulled off his trainers, socks, T-shirt and shorts. Standing naked, his bullish, powerful body seemed vulnerable.

Kate grinned a little self-consciously. 'All right.'

She was rather less sensual in the nude, thought Sean, as he slowly took his own clothes off. Her breasts hung flaccid and the flesh on her thighs was wrinkled.

Diving in, he swam the length of the pool underwater, opening his eyes to see Eric and Kate's legs waving like pale fronds above him. He thought of the kiss again and the deliberation of Eric's tongue. Panic caught at him.

Sean surfaced and found that Eric and Kate had climbed out of the pool and were sitting on the side, dangling their legs in the water. They were both tanned and he wondered how many times they went to 'sunny Spain' and more importantly exactly what they did there.

'I'll get us some drinks.' Without waiting for a reply, Eric began to jog towards the house, as if he was suddenly anxious to leave them behind. For a sordid moment, Sean wondered if he had gone to masturbate.

There was a moment of uneasy silence until Kate asked, 'So you're coming to Spain?'

'Apparently. I don't understand this driving business though.'

'No? The task seems obvious enough to me.'

'Eric hasn't mentioned it before.'

'You worked for Vi?'

'Briefly.'

'You must be traumatised.' Kate suddenly seemed to be unexpectedly understanding.

'That's a good way of putting it.'

'And now you're working for Eric – '

'Am I?'

'Eric always plays his cards close to his chest. Taking over the business at a time like this is quite a responsibility. Confidence has never been one of his strong points.' She seemed much more reasonable now – if also surprisingly frank.

'I hadn't noticed.'

'Eric's always been a loner. Vi saw to that.'

'She rejected him, I gather.'

Kate frowned. 'It's not something I want to talk about,' she said, but Sean felt she had deliberately wrong-footed him. 'Let's just say Eric got the thin end of the wedge, particularly after Andrew died.'

Vi had certainly been a wedge, Sean thought involuntarily, but he didn't make any further comment.

Kate gazed at him expectantly. 'Eric got on with his dad though.'

'That's how he got control of the business, is it?'

'Vi would have been furious, but even she couldn't persuade Fred to cut him out.'

'Who do you think killed them?'

'I wish I knew.'

There was a long, uncomfortable silence.

'What do you do?' Sean knew he was beginning to ask too many questions again.

'I'm in airline catering, a director of Air Gourmet. Eric reckons it's a growth industry. That's how we met. On a plane.' She laughed affectionately, but Sean wondered if she was setting up a scenario – just as he had. 'We were sitting next to each other, both on business. We got talking and I told him I had this little apartment on the Costa Brava. Eric came on a visit and we haven't looked back since.'

'I wonder if you can satisfy my curiosity about something?' asked Sean hesitantly, hoping he wasn't sounding too artificial.

'Try me.'

'Am I following a long line of drivers?'

'You're the first he's had.'

'I wonder why.'

'Eric's a rich man now. I suppose he reckons he can afford a little luxury. How do you feel about that?'

'I'm not sure. When are we going to Spain?'

'Tomorrow.'

13

That evening, Eric and Kate went out for dinner, leaving Sean to wander Fish Pie Island. As he pushed his way through dense foliage he discovered a rotting jetty with a half-sunk Thames cruiser alongside. Dragonflies hovered over the sodden planking and sagging deck while a moorhen, disturbed from its sanctuary, paddled away down a narrow tributary that was overhung with willow trees.

Sean heard the distant hooting of a passing steamer and realised the broad sweep of the Thames must be on the other side of the island. He sat down in the long grass, listening to the glugging sound of the water as it shifted inside the hull.

On the bow of the cruiser he could still make out the faint legend *Green Lady*. Once she must have been sleek and handsome, and judging by the flecks of flaking paint a rich dark green. A hint of varnish and weed-hung brass remained, while a faded, torn pennant fluttered from her prow. On the rotting sun deck was the wooden frame of a deckchair.

Sean had the sudden urge to own and repair her, but recognised immediately that he had yet again slipped back into being Danny. He hesitated, and then decided that for once he had to take a break from the rigours of his new identity.

Danny began to day-dream, seeing himself working on the *Green Lady*, making her sufficiently river-worthy to be towed down to a boatyard. There he would restore the cruiser to her former beauty and they would explore the Thames together, nosing into creeks and tributaries, mooring up beside meadows, motoring broad reaches, queuing at locks, nodding to other boat-owners but never getting into conversation with anyone.

Suddenly, without trying to repress the idea, Danny imagined being joined by Abbie, Rik and Mary, chugging down the Thames together, the river bright and beautiful in the early morning sunlight.

> 'All things bright and beautiful,
> All creatures great and small;

All things wise and wonderful,
The Lord God made them all.'

Tears came into his eyes as he remembered Mary singing the solo at a school concert, and immediately the water became dark and violent, hurtling the *Green Lady* towards a weir. He heard the rending crash of the car again and again, saw the obscene football bounce on to his lap.

The familiar slopping sound inside the water-logged cruiser penetrated Sean's consciousness and he sat up with a dull ache in his head. Had he been asleep? Although he could barely see in the fading light, he could just pick out the silhouette of the torn pennant and the outline of the broken deckchair.

The weir. The terrible image returned as he heard the faint murmur of water, and Sean knew he couldn't return to the emptiness of the house. Instead, he made up his mind to go to the other side of the island, find the bridge and walk up the towpath.

He rose to his feet, his leg muscles protesting, and stiffly began to push through the dense foliage, trying to find the trail he had made. He couldn't, and for a while he was lost amongst the ferns and brambles, almost falling into a scummy pond. Skirting the borders he tried again, disturbing a pair of ducks which flapped noisily across the water.

Several times Sean tried different routes, but all of them seemed to bring him back to the treacherous banks of the pond as an owl hooted in the darkness, mocking his every effort.

He panicked, tried yet another direction, and to his intense relief suddenly broke through into the hay field with the dark, glinting water of the swimming pool. He paused, gasping for air. What the hell was the matter with him? Had he really let Eric Cole get to him so much? The squash match. The fight. The kiss. The phrases repeated themselves over and over again. It was as if Eric had captured him somehow, springing a trap he couldn't struggle out of, as if the wilderness island itself was a prison.

Sean tried to pull himself together and failed, breaking into a run, sprinting past the house and through more dense under-growth towards the bridge that led to the mainland.

Once he had crossed and started walking down the tow-path on the other side, Sean's depression deepened. Without warning, both his identities seemed to slip away and he experienced a devastating sense of emptiness.

'Don't think of Danny. Whatever you do, don't think of him. Not at any time. It's the greatest trap you could fall into. Forget the past and concentrate on the present. Not even day-by-day, make it hour-by-hour. Don't let Danny through.'

But at the moment neither Sean nor Danny seemed to be present as he stumbled blindly on, drawn by the sound of roaring water.

When he reached the lock he walked across the narrow planking of the gate and into the shadow of a cottage, peering through the uncurtained window as he passed. A family was grouped around a TV set and his sense of loss deepened.

Abruptly turning away and carrying on down the tow-path, he eventually came to the wall of water that was the weir, a white torrent in the pale moonlight. He strolled out on to the walkway, looking down at the maelstrom. All he had to do was to scramble astride the safety rail and launch himself off. Wouldn't that be better than fantasising about the *Green Lady* or contemplating a life that never touched anyone, or going to Spain with a games-playing crook who wanted his body?

Real determination seized him, a sweeping desire to plunge into the weir, to find oblivion where there was no memory, no pretence, no danger, no uncertainty. Hopefully, in a few seconds, Danny and Sean could be one. Not wanting the desire to fade, he grabbed the rail and pulled himself up so that he was sitting astride the narrow wooden balustrade.

Now the roaring of the weir seemed louder, even welcoming. It would be easy. There was no need to hesitate so why was he doing so? He didn't want to hang on to life. He had nothing left; Danny had destroyed everything that was precious to him in one careless moment and as for Sean, he wasn't worth a second's consideration. So *why* was he hesitating?

'Come down.' The voice was steady, resolute. 'Like now.'

Sean felt his ankles firmly grasped and realised he was being held by Eric Cole. For a moment he pulled away, but the grip tightened until he allowed himself to be guided back, his hands grasping the damp wood. As Eric let go he jumped down, feeling acutely embarrassed.

'What the hell were you up to?'

'I don't know.'

'Were you going to jump?'

'Maybe.'

'You don't know?'

'How did you manage to creep up on me like that?'

'You were rather preoccupied. I saw you walking up the towpath and thought I'd follow. Lucky I did.'

'I sometimes get low,' Sean said inadequately.

'Is there something you haven't told me?'

He shook his head.

'Come *on*.'

'It's just that I don't seem to have much of a future.'

'You might have an excellent one. What is it about you that's so empty?'

'Thanks.'

'I didn't mean it like that. You have no history. You appeared from nowhere.'

Now they were on really dangerous ground and Sean couldn't think of anything to say. Then he had a mental image of Vi at Runnymede, waiting for her tea.

'That's what your mother liked about me,' he said hastily. 'That I hadn't been around, that I wasn't part of someone else's business.'

'She was naïve.'

'She took a risk.'

'Tell me something about yourself. Anything.' They were facing each other on the narrow walkway, raising their voices against the thundering of the water. Why don't we go somewhere we can bloody hear ourselves think, wondered Sean.

'My parents are dead.'

'How?'

'Road crash. Then I went to South Africa to bum around.' That was an unfortunate word, he thought. Was that what Eric *really* wanted? His arse?

'How did you end up?'

'As a member of the secret police.' Sean was beginning to rally.

'That wasn't such a bad job. What did you have to do for them?'

'Surveillance.'

'And you found the work monotonous?'

'I found it dangerous.'

'So you came back and fell into my mother's arms.'

'Not quite. I hung around some boozers and kept my ear to the ground.'

'You'd made up your mind to be a loser?'

'Didn't seem a lot of choice – '

'What did your parents do?'

'Dad did bent motors and Mum was in the office.'

'He owned a garage?'

'Coachworks. Back-street lock-ups. Strictly small-time.'

Now all Kieron's training was smoothly returning. Thank God for him and his relentless repetition.

'Where did you go to school?'

'Clapham High.'

'Regular attender?'

'Regular bunker.'

It was like the fight. But Sean knew that so far they were only sparring.

'And then?'

'Royal Engineers. I was in Cyprus for a while.'

'And?'

'I left the army. Started up as a demolition contractor. Then Mum and Dad got killed.'

'And you went to South Africa. Whereabouts?'

'Cape Town.'

'How long?'

'Five years.'

'What did you expect to do when you got back here?'

'Not a lot.'

'Ambitious, are you, Sean?'

He shrugged.

'Mum thought a lot of you. According to Dad.'

'Did she?'

'In the very limited time she employed you.' Eric paused. 'Of course if you *had* been ambitious, you could have killed her. Maybe I'm not the only one who enjoys playing games.'

'Why hire me then?'

'To keep an eye on you.'

'Thanks.'

'I still can't make you out.'

'No?'

'Why try and top yourself?'

'I told you – I've got no future.'

'But I've just offered you a job.'

'You never told me.'

'I'm sorry. Here's the formal request. I'd like you to do some driving for me.'

'Can't you do it yourself?'

'I don't want to.'

'Why not?'

'I've got things to think about and I can't concentrate on driving at the same time.'

'What things?'

'Life. Bit like you, except I don't want to start jumping into weirs. Not at my age anyway. When Mum died – when my parents were killed – I didn't know what the hell to do.' Eric was speaking fast now, his words tumbling over each other, as if he didn't want to dwell on any of them. 'When I realised I'd got the business I was gob-smacked. It's a lot of responsibility.' He paused and Sean looked at him curiously, for some reason convinced Eric was telling the truth for once.

'You said you loved your mother?' Sean asked, deliberately going off at a tangent. He could play games too, he thought with savage triumph.

'I had no chance when Andrew was around, but I *didn't* turn him on. He didn't need any help from me. He was in the shit already.'

'Vi was determined to believe you did.'

Eric frowned. 'I know. I could never make her think otherwise. But I still longed to make her happy, still tried to make her love me.' He shook his head and then changed the subject abruptly. 'Look, I can't tell you what I need you to do, not yet. But if you hang in there, I'll make it worth your while.'

For the first time Eric appeared to be more straightforward, even sincere. Sean wondered if this was the case, or was he lying? Answering stroke with stroke. Playing the game even more competitively. It was impossible to say.

'I'd had a few drinks. I guess that's why I got maudlin.' Once again, Sean felt at a disadvantage. Did he really sound so glibly fake?

'I didn't notice the levels had gone down. You must have had some of your own.'

'Checking on me, were you?'

'I'm always alert.'

'Implying?'

'Don't push it. I understand the problem. Leave it at that.'

'You won't tell me what this trip to Spain's about?'

'If I did, we'd both blow it. Just do me a favour and don't believe all my mummy said.' He suddenly sounded enormously bitter but Sean detected grief as well.

'I'll try.'

'We're going tomorrow. That suit? You'll need to be very alert, especially on the road.'

'Is there a problem?'

'There might be.'

Sean slept and dreamt. The *Green Lady* spruce after her loving refit, resplendent with new paint and shining brass, chugged her way down a broad reach of the Thames with Danny at the helm, Abbie in the galley and Rik and Mary quarrelling lazily on the sun deck. He could smell the Sunday roast Abbie was preparing in cramped conditions, the air redolent with the pungency of rosemary and mint, and he could hear her humming to herself.

'When do we make Windsor?' demanded Rik.

'Half an hour.'

'Can I have a go at the helm, Dad?'

'Once we're clear of the lock.'

123

'Can I have a swim when we get there?' asked Mary.

The day was hot and sunny and they waved to the oncoming craft, watching their wakes lap at the tow-path, rocking canoes and dinghies.

Danny could hear the roar of the weir, or was it the traffic on the M25? He knew he hadn't long. He had to hang on to this paradise, to make the most of every second.

He glanced ahead, squinting in the glare of the sun. Then all he could see was a wall of dark water.

Sean woke at 6 a.m., dragged himself out of bed and opened the curtains, gazing through mist towards the grey river and the thundering of the weir. Why had he waited until Eric grabbed his ankles? Why had he allowed himself to be controlled?

As he showered Sean wondered how he was going to operate in Spain. Would Farringdon arrange to have someone contact him? Suppose he wasn't able to trace him? Then he really would be on his own.

Part Three

SUNNY SPAIN

14

Spring sunshine softened the roaring waters of the weir as Sean jogged along the footpath towards the barrier from which he had nearly thrown himself. He leant over the wooden balustrade, gazing down at the water. Would he have survived if he had jumped? The foam on the turbulence flew into the air and a fine spray hovered above the surface, but this morning there was an innocence that he had not recognised before.

He turned round and jogged back to the other side of the island, searching for the line of willows and mossy tributary and overgrown foliage that concealed the *Green Lady*. Eventually Sean found her and gave himself another breather, the dew on the grass soaking his ankles and the smell of the lichen almost soothing after his restless night.

The journey to the airport was incident-free, but was also particularly tense. Eric was withdrawn and silent, but Sean heard Kate whisper, 'I'll keep you safe.'

What on earth did she mean by that? Vi, Elizabeth and Kate. There was a link between them – strength, acumen, leadership – and Sean remembered something Abbie had said. 'Some men need to marry their mother whether they like her or not.'

Eric ordered champagne before lunch on the plane, despite the fact they were in steerage.

Sean had been surprised, assuming that Eric and Kate would travel business class. He was, of course, sitting a row behind them, assuming his rightful position as good and faithful servant. For a while he had slept and then woke wondering what Kate had meant when she had whispered to Eric, 'Don't worry. I'll keep you safe.' He watched them for a moment and felt a stab of loss. Kate had leant her head against Eric's shoulder just as Abbie had when she was tired. He stroked her hair and Sean closed his eyes against it all, keeping them closed until he felt a hand on his knee. Eric was squatting down beside him, holding a route map.

'When we clear Customs at Girona, we go to the Hertz desk and pick up a Fiat Punto. Then you'll drive us to Estartit, which will take about an hour.' He gave him the map. 'I've rented rooms above a restaurant, and we're going to use the same venue for the meeting.'

'What happens afterwards?' Sean tried to recover himself, but he was sure he was sounding deeply artificial. 'A trip on the family yacht? Black Jack at the casino? Aqua-diving?'

'We go back to dear old home sweet home.'

'As simple as that?'

'I hope so.' Suddenly the strain showed in his face and, once again, Sean was reminded of Kate's unexpected reassurance.

'Why couldn't this meeting have been held in the UK? Wouldn't it have been a shade more convenient?'

'Because the guys we're talking to wouldn't be comfortable there.'

'Who are they?'

'You don't have to know that,' said Eric dismissively, and Sean felt a wave of intense irritation.

'Tell me something.'

'If I can.'

'OK, so I'm doing the driving. What else?'

'I thought you might be useful in – any crisis we come up against.'

'Haven't I got rather a poor track record?'

'You've had some good training.'

'What kind of crisis are you expecting?'

'I don't know yet.'

'You trust me then?'

'No way.'

'So you're hoping I trip myself up?'

'That might be the icing on the cake.'

'I don't have a weapon, remember?'

'I can arrange for that if necessary.'

'Even if it puts you at risk?'

'I try to avoid risks like that.'

'But you have to take them.'

'Occasionally. I'm on a learning curve though.'

'What about?'

'You.'

Girona was a small airport, only open in the summer to handle charter flights. Sean walked across the concourse, surrounded by some early holiday-makers bound for fun in the sun, eagerly awaited by fixed-smile couriers from the travel companies who would soon have them trundled away to cheap hotels in coaches with *Hasta La Vista* on the tape deck. Groups milled dependently around their couriers who were holding up little flags as if rallying troops for battle.

'I'm going to take a leak,' said Eric. 'The champagne tells.'

'I'll go too.' Kate was holding his hand. 'I'm a big girl now, so I can just manage with only one male escort.'

Sean was glad they had slipped into this glib and bantering relationship which gave them more space and less opportunity for discord – as if they had both agreed to paper over the cracks.

'Hurry back.'

'Now who's nanny?' demanded Kate. She and Eric disappeared into the crowd, still holding hands, forcibly reminding Sean once again of Vi and Fred, walking slowly through the empty car-park towards the Lily of the Valley.

The woman in the Hertz uniform was English, tanned and middle-aged. Her badge stated her name was Rita. She had a flat bonhomie. 'Your car's ready, sir.'

'I'm just waiting for friends.'

'The weather's been good. Where are you heading for?'

'Estartit.'

'Do you know what you're doing?'

Rita spoke softly, so softly that Sean asked incredulously, 'I'm sorry. What did you say?'

'Do you know what you're doing?'

For a moment he thought she was questioning his ability to drive. Did he look that much of a moron? Then he realised the question might just have some other meaning.

'I can turn you round.' She was standing behind the desk and speaking even more quietly – so quietly that he had to lean forward and incline his head to hear her.

'Setting up as an astrologist, are you?' Sean asked, hoping the extraordinary statements were the merry quips of a rather unorthodox Hertz desk clerk, all of which Rita had at first promised not to be.

'I gave up reading tea-leaves a long time ago. Let's just say we've got an interest in keeping you alive.'

'Who's "we"?'

'I also represent Belling Properties.'

'Moonlighting, are you?'

'It's Vi and Fred's business.'

'I've never heard that name before.'

'You weren't with them very long, were you?'

'Is this a friendly warning, or have you booby-trapped the car?'

'We wouldn't want to give Hertz a bad reputation.'

'So why are you so anxious about my welfare?'

'Vi wouldn't have wanted you working for Eric. If you could just step into the office and sign a few forms, my colleague will look out for your friends.'

The office was chilly and dark with plastic chairs, a smell of pine disinfectant and a rental agreement on a stained table. Sean was considerably shocked. He had thought Eric was the only games player. Just what kind of rival team had been waiting out here for him?

'Do take a seat.' Rita sat down opposite him and pushed the forms across the table. 'I've marked the sections you need to sign.'

Sean sat down and did the paperwork, the after-effects of the lunchtime champagne beginning to tell. His mouth was dry and his hand shook as he tried to work out some kind of strategy. But his mind remained blank.

'Remember how fond Vi was of you? Make a decision. Go home.'

'Eric wouldn't like that.'

'He wouldn't be able to do much about it. You'd be in the VIP lounge, waiting for a business class flight back to the UK.'

'No fun in the sun?'

'The sun can be fatal.'

'I'm afraid I'm keen on my fun.'

'That's a pity.'

Sean stood up and glanced through the open door into the concourse. 'I don't see my friends.'

'I expect they'll be here soon.' Rita was soothing now.

'They've been away a long time.'

'Maybe someone's got a stomach problem.'

'It's a bit early for that. Why didn't you contact me in England?'

'We didn't have the chance.'

Sean closed the door gently.

Rita gazed at him thoughtfully.

'Who told you to warn me off?'

'Someone who's concerned about your safety.'

The phone rang, saving them both from the impasse.

She picked up the receiver, listened with some relief, and then said, 'He's with me now.' Rita passed the phone over the table to him. 'Have a word,' she said. 'I think the lady might make more sense than me.'

'Sean?'

The voice was instantly familiar but he couldn't immediately identify it.

'Vi wouldn't have liked you travelling with Eric.'

'I thought I'd see what kind of guy he was.'

'Curiosity killed the cat. It might kill you too.'

Then he knew. Of course he knew. Why hadn't he recognised her voice immediately? Sean could see her now, standing in the rain outside the church.

'Elizabeth – '

'That's me.'

'You told me you had nothing to do with the business.'

'Did I?'

'You know damn well you did,' he lied, deliberately trying to unsettle her.

'The directors invited me to step into the breach. A woman's hand is often steadier at the helm.'

'But Eric's in charge now. How come he's putting up with you?'

'He doesn't have to. I represent a group who don't like Eric Cole taking over. We represent Vi.'

'What do you want?'

'She left me a bit of money and I'm just trying to put it to good use.'

'What sort of use?' said Sean.

'Trying to stop Eric selling us up the Swannee.'

'How's he going to do that?'

'We think he has a meeting with Midas.'

'I see.' Sean felt that he was getting somewhere at last.

'He could sell the business without them having to take over – and spill more blood.'

'*Midas* killed them all?'

'Or Eric.'

'So why try and get rid of me?'

'You're in a dangerous position. Vi wouldn't want that. Neither do we.'

'I'm not going back.'

'I see.' There was a long silence. Then Elizabeth said slowly, 'If you're determined to stick with him – are you prepared to work for Vi as well?'

'Why are you playing games with me? I thought that was Eric's prerogative.'

'I've watched his games since he was in the cradle.'

'So you're simply following in a tradition.'

'I'm using his own weapon against him. Clever old Auntie Liz.' She paused and then said, 'We need to assess the stakes.'

'So why try to get me back to the UK?'

'We didn't think you'd have the bottle to work for us. We've already got someone tailing Eric. But you could be useful back-up.'

'So what do you want me to do?'

'I'll be in touch.' She laughed and then coughed, and Sean could almost see her lighting up yet another fag while she was talking to him.

He put down the phone, realising he had just become something of a double agent.

132

15

'You've been away a long time.'

Eric and Kate sauntered across the concourse arm-in-arm, as if they needed to broadcast their solidarity.

'I met someone I knew – an old business acquaintance.' Eric seemed slightly agitated. 'I just stopped for a quick chat.'

'I was wondering what had happened to you. I've signed all the papers and got the car keys.' Sean was reproving.

'We'd better get going then.' Eric seemed tense and irritable as they walked in silence towards the exit.

Sean put his foot down, automatically taking the Punto into the fast lane as he thought over the alarming new development. Was Elizabeth really acting for Vi, or had she sprung a trap? Whose game was it? Eric's? Elizabeth's? Vi's?

Sean's attention abruptly returned to the present as he glanced down at the dashboard and saw that he was speeding.

Not so fast.

Go for it, Dad.

Listen to Mum.

The pain from the past was so great that he almost lost control, and with brakes screaming, he suddenly veered from the fast lane to the slow.

'What in Christ's name are you doing?' shouted Eric. 'Trying to kill us?'

I did that before. The phrase repeated itself in his mind. *I did that before.*

'What's going on?' demanded Kate.

Sean sought desperately for some kind of reason for his erratic behaviour. 'I thought I saw someone on that bridge back there. But I must have been wrong.'

'You saw someone on the bridge,' snapped Kate. 'Does that require changing lanes at high speed?'

'I'm sorry.'

Eric, however, was more ameliorating. He also sounded curious. 'Let's get this straight. You saw someone threatening us?'

'I thought they had a gun. But I'm jumpy and I fucked up. What else can I say?'

'We're both jumpy.'

Again, the feeling of uneasy intimacy, of almost being covered up for.

'I hope you guys aren't going to foul up on this,' Kate muttered.

Had she sensed that Eric was protecting him, wondered Sean.

He drove on in silence. Eric had his eyes closed while Kate stared out of the side window as they turned off the motorway and picked up the local road to Palamos.

We're both jumpy. They had both lost their families. Last night Eric had prevented his suicide attempt. It was enough to result in a bonding for life, a bonding that couldn't do either of them any good. Why did Eric really want him so much, wondered Sean. Why had he gone to such elaborate lengths to test him out?

'Wake up, Eric,' said Kate. 'You're not being very good company.' There was more apprehension in her voice than admonishment.

'I'm not asleep.'

'What are you doing then?'

'Taking the liberty of having a think.'

'I'm sorry. I just don't like it when you switch off.'

Why is she so out of character, Sean wondered. Kate was usually so dominant. He had also noticed they were talking as if he wasn't there.

'I was thinking about how we used to go to Estartit as kids.'

'Is that why you set the meeting up there?'

'Julio Puig owns the Mas Coral – the restaurant I told you about with the amazing view across the harbour to the Medas Islands. He's an old friend of my parents.'

'I wish I'd known Fred and Vi better than I did,' said Kate.

Who are you, Sean wondered. He knew as little about her as Eric knew about him. They were all trying to run rings round each other, but he also knew that it had to stay that way.

'Julio used to swim off the rocks with us. I don't think I've ever been so shit-scared in my life. That was my mother's fault.'

'Isn't everything?' Kate laughed to cover up the edge in her voice.

'Very Freudian,' Eric replied. 'She wanted us to reach the patch of blue that was beyond the rocks, out in deep water. The sun always seemed to be shining there.'

'Very symbolic,' said Kate

'Mum always wanted her menfolk to test themselves out.'

'What about her?'

'She couldn't swim.'

'Very convenient.'

'No need to be such a bitch.' But Eric didn't sound particularly annoyed.

'What about Andy dearest? Wasn't she concerned for her beloved's safety?'

'She just knew we'd all have to go through hell to reach her little patch of blue.'

'Was it worth reaching?'

'It was a wonderful feeling. Once we'd all passed Mum's test I'd look back at the waves breaking on the rocks and think, Christ, that was worth it. The water was warm – '

'Like a mother's heart.'

Eric gave Kate an irritable glance and then hurried on. 'I wonder if that patch of blue is still there – or maybe we all imagined it. Mum used to sit on this rock with her knitting and a magazine, and watch us very carefully getting into the water. We got bumped and bruised and cut on the barnacles. Dad and Julio would lead the way and Andy and I would follow. There was this special technique. You had to catch the right wave and let it wash you over the rocks. If you didn't, then you'd get cut to hell.' He was silent for a moment. 'OK, we might have had our differences, Mum and I – bloody great painful differences – but I have to thank the old bitch for passing on all the drive she had.'

'And Julio had to go through your mother's torture too?'

'He's almost family. After all, Dad put a lot of finance into the restaurant and Julio put in his expertise. It's a Michelin three-star now,' Eric ended with childlike triumph.

'I bet Julio never swam off the rocks when the Coles weren't in Estartit.'

'I'm sure you're right, Kate. You taking all this in?' he asked Sean with determined patronage.

Estartit had been over-developed into a jumbled mass of cheap restaurants and souvenir shops, with a harbour that contained a large number of luxury yachts and motor cruisers.

Eventually the wide road running alongside the dusty beach narrowed off into a single track between apartment blocks on the land side and craggy rocks rising from a dark crimson sea.

Sean could see the humped shapes of islands half a mile out which had the timeless quality of barren isolation, despite their proximity to the tawdry resort.

'The Medas,' said Eric. 'Fortunately you can't land there. Dad had a cruiser when we were kids and used to moor up as close as he could. I used to love looking up at the islands, thinking what it would be like to sleep there for the night, wake up at dawn and just sit and watch.'

'Could we get permission to do that?' Kate sounded quite different, far less controlled and without her usual authority, as Sean drove down the side road to the car-park behind the restaurant.

The tables with their crisp white cloths spilled out on to the terrace with its sunset view over the bay.

'Elegant dining on the surf,' muttered Kate.

'With prices to match,' said Eric. 'Julio likes to keep them high,' he added, as Sean pulled the suitcases out of the boot of the Punto.

'So who comes to eat?'

'Locals. Yachtsmen. Julio knows how to run a good restaurant.'

'Just a minute,' said Kate with a return to her old self. 'Put the bags down, Sean.' She turned to Eric. 'I think we should talk some things through out here.'

He nodded and then shrugged. 'The lady's not for waiting.'

'Just give me the blindfold.' Sean was exhausted, but he didn't want to stop the banter which suddenly seemed like a lifeline. 'That wall over there will do.'

136

'What are you on about?'

'This is a discreet place for a firing squad, isn't it? What about the condemned man's last drink though? I'd settle for a gin and tonic.'

Eric gave him a chilly smile. 'A lot depends on the meeting tomorrow. I suggest you try to take your job seriously.'

'I've got a job now, have I? That I didn't know.'

'The meeting could last for some time – a few hours, maybe. You can either take a walk or stay in your room, or even both.'

'Wow!'

'Then we'll have a good dinner – all three of us – which we hope will be a celebration. Early next morning you drive us back to Girona.'

'So far you've succeeded in telling me nothing at all.' Sean could feel his temper rising. 'Why the hell do you want me out here? You could have hired a taxi.'

'We're talking to investors,' said Kate.

'Investing in what? Don't tell me it's airline catering. How much longer are you going to shut me out?'

'Until we can trust you.'

'When will that be?'

'I've really no idea.'

'What do you think I am? Your poodle?' Sean hoped that an angry confrontation might be a short cut. To believe that Eric and Kate were meeting anonymous financiers to agree on an investment in airline catering would be ingenuous, particularly after his telephone conversation with Elizabeth.

'We won't get anywhere by having an argument,' said Kate smugly.

'Why won't you tell me what you're doing? Why you're here?' Sean made himself sound slightly hysterical. Surely no one would blindly follow instructions like this?

'I've told you as much as I can,' Eric intervened.

'I'm talking to Kate.'

'I'm sorry.' She was clearly trying to be reasonable. 'I can't say any more. Not now anyway.'

'Why is an investment in an airline catering company being treated with such secrecy?'

'Because it's a highly competitive business.'

Who is she, wondered Sean yet again, and wondered why

137

Farringdon hadn't mentioned her. Suddenly he became convinced that Kate was in charge and had been all along. If this meeting *was* with Midas, could she be some kind of negotiator?

Sean realised that he had taken the confrontation as far as it could reasonably go – at least for the time being. 'OK,' he muttered. 'I just don't like being isolated.'

'Try thirty years of it!' Eric muttered. 'Then you'll really fucking well know what isolation means.'

16

The Mas Coral was large, with a preponderance of marble, dark woodwork and Spanish tiles. Sean began dinner with langoustine and went on to moules in a delicate, tangy tarragon sauce while the wine flowed. The atmosphere at the table, however, was not conducive to good digestion. The food was consumed in near silence, punctuated by awkward attempts at conversation that burnt themselves out as soon as they were begun.

Later, as liqueurs were served, Julio Puig finally arrived, anxious and forbidding. Tall with a pale, indoor face he was painfully thin and Sean noticed that Eric kept glancing at him curiously.

Eventually he seemed to summon up the courage to hesitantly ask, 'You've lost a lot of weight. Is there anything wrong?'

'I have cancer.'

There was a stunned silence while Sean looked down at his plate, feeling intrusive. It was as if Eric's world was falling apart even more rapidly than his own. Again he felt the bonding.

'You didn't tell me.' Eric was almost angry.

'It's not a matter for the telephone.'

'Or a letter?'

'That too.'

'This is my driver,' said Eric. 'Sean Pollard. He worked for my mother.'

'Vi and Fred were my very good friends.' Julio glanced around him with a sudden satisfaction. 'The Coral wouldn't be here if it wasn't for their generosity. Now I don't know what its future will be. There have been so many – changes.'

'Are you having chemo?' Eric asked abruptly.

'That is not possible. The cancer is in the lymph glands.'

'What are you going to do?'

'I'm going to die.'

The silence that followed seemed unbreakable.

Then Kate asked brutally, 'How long have you got?'

'A few months – maybe less.'

'Are you in much pain?'

'The doctor gives me medication and I drink a lot of good wine.' He paused. 'I don't see any point in discussing the problem as I have no options and my position is terminal. I live for the hour – not even the day.' He brusquely changed the subject. 'Your meeting will be upstairs in our private dining room. Will that be convenient for your – associates?' Julio seemed to show little interest in the meeting and its purpose. 'You'll need lunch served, of course.'

'Thank you,' said Eric. 'Let me know how much it will cost. I'll pay the – '

'No.' Julio looked up. 'It's on the house, as you say.'

'Thank you.'

Another silence followed, eventually broken by Eric.

'Do you remember the patch of blue?'

At first he seemed bewildered. Then Julio smiled with a sudden warmth. 'Your mother's – '

'Patch of blue. Beyond the rocks.' Eric sounded slightly slurred.

'Of course. It was a tough challenge.'

'Can you still swim?'

'I haven't been in the water for years.'

Sean caught Kate's slight smile and remembered what she had said earlier about Julio not having to swim when the Coles weren't at Estartit.

'Tomorrow morning. Early. The weather's been good. We'll have another go and you can sit on the rock and watch – and recall my mother.'

'What a wonderful idea.' Kate was mocking.

'If you don't mind looking at the scar where they opened me up.' To Sean's surprise, Julio was enthusiastic, no longer just the shell of the man he had been. 'I would like to join you.'

'Are you sure? It might hurt – ' Eric looked worried.

'I'll be the judge of that,' said Julio. 'Just as your mother was so often the judge of us.'

'And particularly me,' added Eric.

Kate turned to Sean. 'What about you?'

Did he want to be included, he wondered. Then to his surprise

140

Sean decided that he did. Maybe he needed Vi's approbation as much as they all did.

He was fairly drunk when he went to bed and slept heavily with the shutters closed in the hot dark room. Towards dawn, he dreamt of a vast gnomic labyrinth underneath St Tropez. A conveyor belt of coffins was clanking past until the production line came to a grinding halt as Vi swept in, wearing an outdated but entirely suitable Victorian nightgown.

A gnome approached her with doughnuts on a silver tray. He bowed and Vi received the offering graciously. She then gave an order and the gnome eased four coffins down to the earth floor. As his eyes travelled towards the inscriptions Sean woke with a hangover and lay there for a moment, mulling over his ludicrous dream.

Then he struggled out of bed and on to the cool tiled floor. Opening the windows, he stepped out on to a balcony overlooking the sea and saw mist rising slowly from the islands. A fishing boat chugged out towards them through a lazy swell and he heard the incessant hollow booming of a fog horn.

Then he saw Kate standing on the adjoining balcony, looking strangely vulnerable.

'Let's *do* the balcony scene then,' said Sean brightly as she glared at him.

'You're so fucking ignorant, aren't you? There weren't two balconies, shit-head. Juliet stood on hers while Romeo kept to the ground.'

'Don't let's argue over detail. What have you done with Eric?'

'He's out like a light. I'm not sure he's going to make his patch of blue after all.'

'It's important to him. After all, he's only got a hangover.'

'Is that what you call it?' she said angrily. 'As we're on our own, do tell me where your aspirations really lie.'

'I don't get you.'

'Are you queer?'

'For Christ's sake!' He was completely thrown.

'Are you a fag? A faggot. A jumped-up little arse licker?'

'All charges denied.' He tried unsuccessfully to return to the banter.

141

'I thought you would have sussed that Eric's bent.'

'I still don't see what you're on about.' Sean needed time. He also knew he needed to be extremely careful.

'Are you thick or something?' she suddenly shouted, startling a man on a clanking black bicycle who gazed up at their balcony scene with shaky interest as he pedalled past. 'Don't you understand what I'm telling you, for Christ's sake? Eric is bisexual. He likes to fuck with men and women – '

'The point is, had *you* sussed it out?'

Kate stared back at Sean, her hostility increasing. 'I was suspicious.'

'And . . .'

'Last night I was sure.'

'How long have you known him?'

'For some time.'

'And yet you've only just realised that?'

'I worked with his brother. Then Eric joined us.'

'Did you have a relationship with Andrew?'

'No. We were colleagues.'

'In airline catering. I didn't know he was interested in that – although it's a growth industry of course, isn't it?'

'So Eric brought you here as a toy-boy.'

'As a driver actually.'

Despite the farcical aspect of having a row on two adjoining balconies which would soon attract the attention of more passers-by, Sean pushed home his advantage. Kate's temper had obviously unempowered her, and for once he was in control.

'So he didn't fuck you last night? Is that what all this is about?'

'I just want to find out if he screws you too.'

'Sorry to disappoint you, but the answer is no.'

'What about the squash court?'

'I was worried about that.'

'Isn't worried rather a weak word?'

'No. What happened was so unexpected that I couldn't cope.'

'I don't want a threesome.'

'You haven't got one.'

'This is a business trip. We'll be talking finance all day so you make yourself scarce. You're a servant, remember?'

'A servant who takes his orders from Eric.'

'Mr Eric to you.'

'Since when?' His sense of power and domination was surging and Sean felt a rush of physical desire for her. 'You're right out of order, aren't you? But I know what this is all about. You're worried that we'll soon be screwing the arse off each other and you're going to be marginalised. So get this, for the last time, I'm heterosexual through and through. The rest of it's all in the mind, isn't it, sweetheart?'

'What are you two on about?' Eric sounded as if he had his head under the sheets.

'Kate and I were just sharing a joke on our respective balconies.'

'I don't feel like sharing jokes.'

'The only thing we should be sharing,' said Kate brightly, 'is a very large Bloody Mary.'

'Get me one then!' groaned Eric.

'Now who's a good and faithful servant?' whispered Sean.

Kate gave him a V sign as she went inside.

Breakfast in the empty restaurant was even more tense and silent than dinner had been the previous night. As Kate crumbled a croissant between her fingers, Sean suddenly realised that he wanted sex with her. Could the bantering that seemed to have led to the row on the balcony have been seductive?

Meanwhile, Eric was ignoring them both, drinking black coffee and turning but barely reading the pages of *El Pais*.

Then Julio appeared, looking even more fragile than he had the previous night.

'There's no need for that swim,' said Eric hurriedly.

'There's every need. I very much want to go.'

Eric folded his paper and scowled at Kate. She looked away and as the waiter began to clear the breakfast plates from the marble tables he stood up. 'By the time we're down at the rocks we should have walked off the croissants.' He was jarringly hearty.

Sean went up to his room, collected his trunks and returned to the gloomy, dark-tiled corridor. As he had hoped, Kate was waiting for him.

'I just wanted to say I was sorry.' She spoke too glibly.

'That's OK.'

'It's not, but it'll have to do.'

'As long as you don't think – '

'I don't know what to think. I just don't want to discuss it. I've apologised. Isn't that enough?'

'Not really.'

'Do you want me to grovel?'

'It might be interesting.'

'Eric's under a lot of strain.' She hesitated. 'He's decided to sell the business.'

'That's the last thing Vi would have wanted.' Sean was surprised to find how indignant he was on her behalf.

'Then he's running true to form – at least that's what she'd think.'

'How well did you know her?'

'Hardly at all. But I didn't like what I saw.'

'What about Fred?'

'She ran him.'

'Like you run Eric?'

'How did you get that impression?'

Sean didn't answer directly. 'Why are you the go-between? You always seem to have an early copy of the script.'

'Eric never wants to give anything away.'

'But he doesn't mind if you do?'

'Perhaps I'm cut out to be your go-between.'

'Like you are between Eric and the investors?'

'I never said that.' She was wary now.

'Could they be buying the business rather than investing in it? Is that why Eric's so anxious?'

'Is he? I'd just describe him as severely hung-over.'

It's stalemate, thought Sean, and was sure Kate felt the same, although he could also sense the sexual desire increasing between them. 'If he sells the business, what's he going to do?'

'He'll be a partner in mine. At least it's a little more orthodox, don't you think? Eric would be better off without his more dubious connections.'

'Like me?'

'Are you saying you *are* a dubious connection?'

144

'While we're on the subject, what about these investors? Are they Midas?'

'Why do you ask?' Kate was even more wary now.

'Vi told me.'

'Do you know what Midas is?' she sneered.

'An illegal international monetary fund that finances terrorism and runs large-scale criminal organisations. Like Vi and Fred's.'

'You've got that off pat, haven't you? Vi was paranoid and a particularly stupid woman. She always was a small-time criminal.'

'Not so small. In stature – or influence.'

Kate looked at her watch. 'We've got to go. I'm sorry we can't indulge in any more sharing and caring.'

'So my role hasn't changed? I'm just here for the ride.'

'Eric and I aren't sure.'

'What's that meant to mean?' Sean felt a sudden chill.

She smiled, knowing she'd scored. 'You say Eric's hired you as a driver, but suppose . . .' She paused for effect. '. . . you'd attached yourself to him for some other purpose? That would be a bit of a how-do-you-do, wouldn't it?'

Sean shrugged. 'Vi found my credentials held up.'

'She would, wouldn't she? She could have taken a wrong decision. After all, Vi spent most of her life making wrong decisions. Particularly about Eric.'

Sean had the distinct feeling that Kate had grabbed back any advantage he might have gained.

The sea was a deep, meridian blue as the waves pounded the promontory, spray sweeping the barnacle-encrusted rocks.

'Once you're out there,' said Eric, 'you're safe.'

Sean could see Vi now, sitting, knitting, watching her menfolk take on the elements, no doubt feeding her face at the same time. He wondered if doughnuts were readily available in Spain.

'That's the best way to get in.'

Sean followed Eric's gaze. A sharp cleft in the rock led down to a pool that was continuously filled by surf. When each wave withdrew, there was a few seconds' gap before the next surge.

'You have to move fast. Wait till the wave's cresting and then

145

scramble down as if there's no tomorrow. Swim through the pool, get out the other side and launch yourself off. Then go like hell.'

The heat was intense, the sky pressing down menacingly, and the water was a dark seething mass – but the patch of blue lay beyond.

Although Sean was highly apprehensive, he was also conscious that he had to prove himself yet again. 'I'll go first,' he said uneasily.

But Eric was not going to have his leadership challenged. 'No way. You need to see how it's done.'

Julio, pale and emaciated in a pair of boxer shorts, a livid scar across his stomach, backed him up. 'You watch, señor. This is tough.'

Sean felt thoroughly patronised yet again, and when he glanced up at Kate she gave him a triumphant smile.

'I assume you haven't done this before either?' he asked her.

'Of course she hasn't.' Eric seemed to be on the edge of losing his temper. 'But she's a damned fine swimmer.'

'Damn good show then,' replied Sean maliciously.

He watched the swirling water withdraw and the next crest gather while Eric clambered with considerable agility down the uneven surface of the rock, slipping and floundering across the pool just as a wave came surging in. Standing up on a ledge, he dived and then surfaced the other side, swimming powerfully towards the patch of blue.

Julio watched, waited and plunged. Surprisingly, despite his frailty, he had even more expertise and didn't have to dive through the wave for the surge hadn't yet reached the rocks.

Kate followed with equal skill, the sun turning the three of them momentarily golden.

Sean screwed his eyes up against the dazzle which made the oncoming crests difficult to see.

Concentrating hard, he watched a wave rebound on itself. Sean still couldn't see the water level in the pool clearly, but knew he had to take a decision. Clambering down the rock face he stumbled, losing his footing, going under and then surfacing again. At first he couldn't make out who was shouting, but then he heard Eric, louder than the others.

'Not now. Go back!'

Ignoring the advice, despite the fact that he knew he was too late, Sean swam as hard as he could, but the wave surged into the pool and he found himself being hurled back, his shoulders making painful contact with barnacle-encrusted rock.

Then, as the wave began to withdraw, Sean was dragged out with the current until he found himself being lacerated by the vicious surface of the rocks on the other side. He clung to them, pale blood on his hands and chest, until with a monumental effort he got a foothold just as the next crest roared towards him. Somehow he managed to stand up, making a toppling dive into the heaving sea.

Swearing as the salt found his wounds, Sean reached his patch of blue.

'Now look what you've done. Eric told you to wait,' admonished Kate. 'I'll put something on those shoulders when we get out. I brought a first-aid kit in my bag – just in case.'

Just in case I can patronise you again, Sean thought savagely.

They were treading water in a small circle, the sunlight giving each of them a fiery halo that glinted and glowed.

'I cocked it up,' Sean gasped.

'Let's hope that's all you cock up,' snapped Eric.

But Julio was impatient. 'What's with you guys? This is meant to be fun, isn't it? Why are the British so competitive?'

Kate caught Sean's eye and then looked away again.

They made a triumphant circle in the heaving swell and then swam apart, treading water, watching the waves thunder at the rocks.

'I know what you're thinking,' said Eric.

'What *am* I thinking?'

'That we have to go back the same way.'

'I expect I'll manage.'

'No need. We'll swim round the point. There's a more

comfortable landing there.' He turned to look at Vi's rock. 'I can still see Mum, sitting up there with her fucking knitting. I often wondered if she hoped I'd drown. I reckon her spirit's still there, watching me now.'

'Hoping you'll drown?' asked Sean innocently.

He floated on his back, the salt still stinging painfully. But Vi had been right. The patch of blue had definitely been worth reaching. The water was warm and the swell rocked him like a baby in a cradle.

Then he heard a familiar dull thud, and turning over on his front Sean saw a car was turning round on the track under the cliffs at high speed.

'For Christ's sake, dive!' He began to swim towards Eric in a fast crawl, sure he was too late. 'Dive, you fucking idiot!' he yelled over the roar of the waves, but they drowned his words. 'Dive!'

For a moment Eric seemed not to hear him, swimming towards Julio who was floating on his back with his eyes closed. Kate, back in the patch of blue, was lazily drifting.

'What are you on about?' asked Eric.

'For fuck's sake, dive!'

Sean saw the pale blood in the next crest and knew the bullet had already found a target. Meanwhile, the car, an unmistakable Renault Twingo, was speeding away in a dusty cloud, narrowly avoiding a Peugeot.

He tried to read the number plate, but it was too far away.

'Sean.' Kate gave a choking cry. 'For God's sake.'

'What is it?'

Eric surfaced, spluttering.

Julio's head was thrown back and Sean could see the ragged tear just below his hairline, the blood gushing into the swell in a red swathe.

He swam over to him as fast as he could, putting Julio in a life-saving position, feeling for his pulse while the others trod water, trying to come to terms with what had happened.

'That was meant for me,' Eric observed bleakly.

17

The breakers were pounding the rocks more ferociously as the wind freshened, and Julio's corpse was now in danger of being swept away.

'We've got to get him out,' yelled Eric.

'I'll do that.' Sean began to pull Julio towards the shore. His body was colder now and seemed to be heavier as he fought his way around the headland towards the shelving rock behind the reef.

'We'll land him here. I'll need to make sure he doesn't get ripped apart by those fucking barnacles.'

'He's dead,' Kate shouted.

'Does *that* matter?'

With Kate and Eric pulling from above and Sean pushing from below, Julio's body was dragged on to the rock without damage.

As people began to run over the uneven surface towards them, Eric grabbed Sean's arm. 'I'm sorry.'

'It's terrible.'

'Not just about Julio.'

'What then?'

'Don't you realise? You've passed the final test, for Christ's sake. Now I know you can be trusted.'

'It had to take all this?'

The police and paramedics arrived within minutes, pushing through the vicarious crowd, and as Julio's corpse was zipped into a body-bag, Sean began to explain to a Spanish police officer where the shot had come from while Eric and Kate stood by helplessly in the blazing sun.

'Did Señor Puig have enemies?' The question was directed at Eric.

'You'll have to ask the staff in the restaurant. All I know is that he was an old friend of my family – and he was recently diagnosed as having cancer. None of that exactly makes for enemies.'

The police officer nodded impatiently. 'He was also gay.'

Sean watched Kate's face but her expression remained blank.

'He wasn't in the least predatory,' said Eric.

'He didn't have a partner – '

'Not for some years. He'd got used to living alone.'

'You're here on a visit?'

'We've come for a business meeting.'

'What kind of business meeting?'

'My friend – Kate Bradman – she's an executive director of an airline catering company. We're talking to some associates about investment.'

'And this man?'

'He's my driver. Sean Pollard.'

'You knew Julio Puig well?'

'Yes, but my parents knew him better.'

'Who are they?'

'Violet and Fred Cole,' Eric replied uncomfortably, and then paused expectantly. But when the police officer made no comment he added, 'I very much fear that I could have been the target.'

'Why didn't you tell me that before?'

'I'm sorry. As you'll understand, this has been a terrible shock. My parents were murdered just a couple of weeks ago.'

'How?'

'Their house was bombed.'

'And what was their connection with Julio?'

'I told you. They were family friends.'

The police officer's expression suddenly changed to a look of increasing excitement and curiosity, as if this background information had put Eric into some kind of different league. 'I remember now. I read about the death of your parents in the English newspapers. What was their work?'

'Property.'

'The newspapers seemed to think differently. They said they were criminals.'

'Only the tabloids would print that.'

'Then their servants were killed. Is that right? Now, a few days later one of their old friends is murdered – '

'I've already told you I think the shot was meant for me – '

'We have no wish for English criminals to bring their problems to Spain. It is bad enough with your football hooligans.'

The sanctimonious comment was unanswerable.

'Where are you staying?'

'In rooms above the Mas Coral.'

'You may not be able to leave tomorrow. I shall need to speak to you for a longer time. Much longer. I will come to the restaurant later. Please make sure you're there.'

'We shan't be going anywhere.'

'I am sorry about Julio Puig. He was a successful restaurateur – a credit to Estartit.'

'He was a credit to my family as well,' said Eric.

The three of them walked back to the Mas Coral in silence, the shock bonding them together, and Sean experienced a new sense of belonging. As he glanced at Eric he could hardly believe his good fortune for fate had clearly dealt him a major advantage.

'I'll have to break the news to the staff,' Eric said.

'I'll help you.' Kate was almost subservient. 'If you want me to.'

'They probably know already.'

Sean had no idea whether this was the right moment or not, but he knew he had to try to move forward. 'So you can trust me now?' he asked hesitantly.

'I'm sorry it took so long. But you can understand why I had so many doubts.'

'I'm glad you took me along.'

'For the ride?' Kate asked, clearly not able to take the self-congratulatory exchange.

Eric swept on. 'It was the only way to suss you out, wasn't it?'

'I assume the meeting isn't about in-flight catering.' They had come to a halt outside an ice-cream parlour which also adver-tised 'All-Day English Breakfast'. A group of young British tourists, hung-over from the lager of the night before, red-faced from the unaccustomed sun, their skin peeling, were consuming rubbery fried eggs and soggy-looking bacon.

152

'We could take a few minutes.' Eric glanced round and led them over to a café, raucous with live music. He ordered beers and while they were waiting for them to arrive he turned to Kate. 'All right?'

'I think we might find Sean useful after all.'

'My mother was right when she told you I did drugs,' said Eric. 'And I do them big.'

The news was an even greater shock than Julio's death and Sean was surprised and deeply regretful. He had hoped that Vi's prejudice might be disproved. Unfortunately she had been dead right.

18

'Gatwick?' asked Sean in a monotone.

'We have a network of baggage handlers, ground staff, air crew, even Customs officers. But now we want to double the imports and it's going to cost us.'

The beers arrived and Eric took a long draught.

'I can see how disappointed you are. Well – maybe I disappoint myself.'

'So Vi was right and you'd set up your own little earner?'

'Correct.'

'What about your father?'

'I never told him. I wasn't going to kick him in the balls.'

'Particularly if he was going to let you into the business . . .'

'I'd have bled Dad dry siphoning off a major investment in Gatwick. Anyway, I'd have trouble with the rank and file.'

Sean thought of Elizabeth. He didn't think she would appreciate being the rank and file. He also wondered just how much trouble Eric had been expecting and suspected he had underestimated the extent.

'I need outside cash – and fast.' He gazed at two children running down the beach with buckets and spades, intent and purposeful. 'My mother was waiting for me to prove myself a shit,' he added reflectively.

'Did Julio know?'

Eric laughed. 'He certainly did. He was my contact out here.'

'On the drug scene?'

'He'd been an associate of my parents for so long that no one suspected his additional interests.'

'How did Julio come over to your way of thinking?' asked Sean.

'Money.'

'And who killed him?'

'Do you think Elizabeth could still be trying to protect my mother's financial interests?'

*

Sean hoped he hadn't given himself away, but it was difficult to keep up with what Eric knew. But after all, surely it was only a process of elimination? No friend of Vi's could possibly be a friend of his.

'Did you know her?' asked Eric guardedly.

'I met her once – but your mother never mentioned her to me.'

'The funeral?'

'How do you know?'

'It wasn't exactly clandestine.'

'She was only venting her spleen.'

'Elizabeth's good at that. What was she on about?'

'She was saying your mother should never have treated you the way she did. So on that basis, why should she be representing her interests?'

'Money. Just like Julio. There's people in the business who resent the way I've gained control. And I'm sure my mother resented even the possibility that this could happen. Maybe she set Auntie Liz up to be her avenging angel.'

'I don't like the implication,' said Sean.

'That doesn't mean to say I killed her.'

'What does it mean to say?'

'That my mother was always far-sighted – much more so than Dad.'

'Who do you think *did* kill them then?'

'I wish to God I knew. I'm going to need some real protection now. How do you fancy me getting you a snub-nosed automatic?' Eric attempted a Chandler gangster drawl which didn't work. Sean wondered just how much he regretted Julio's assassination.

'We're talking about Midas, aren't we? Although Kate denies they're involved in this meeting.' Sean glanced at her, interested to see how she would react, but she only contented herself with an admonishing smile. 'They're your "outside help", aren't they?' he persisted. 'So don't you think they're manipulating you?'

'What do you mean?'

'Suppose *Midas* killed Eric's parents – '

'There would be little point in that – '

'Let me finish.' The satisfying feeling of taking the initiative

155

returned to Sean. 'Suppose they then murdered Roberto and Maria.'

'Why should they?'

'Maybe they knew something about the planting of the bomb,' he suggested. 'Or maybe they did the planting.'

'They were devoted to my parents,' said Eric dismissively.

'So was Julio.'

'There's a lot of difference between – '

'You said yourself people will do anything for money. Midas seem to have an awful lot to spread around.'

'Who's next in the grand conspiracy?' asked Kate.

'Maybe Midas's plan was to put Eric in charge of the business and then kill him too.'

'The body-count's rising,' said Kate. 'But it wouldn't do them much good, would it?'

'There's nothing like rubbing out the family dynasty to make a nice fresh start. And the business *is* big money, isn't it, Kate?' Sean knew he was scoring again.

'It might just be worth the effort.'

'There's always Elizabeth,' said Eric. 'Why are you discounting her?'

'I'm not.'

Sean wondered if he had actually succeeded in narrowing the possible culprits down. Elizabeth or Midas. Unless, of course, she was actually working for them which would make for a very neat conclusion – except that, in real life, conclusions had an irritating habit of not being neat at all.

'There's only one flaw,' said Kate.

'What's that?'

'I'm a director of Midas and I can guarantee that we weren't involved in your oh-so-convenient conspiracy theory.'

'What evidence have you got?'

'Don't you believe the lady's word?' asked Eric mockingly.

'So when you met Eric on that plane . . .' began Sean, and then deliberately paused.

'Yes?' asked Kate impatiently.

'You didn't see him as a sitting target?'

'That's right out of order.'

Sean was delighted, knowing he had got her on the raw again.

'We've tried to confide in you. So what's the point of being so manipulative?' Kate was satisfyingly furious.

'I'm not your poodle. I think I told you that before.'

'Could be the dog has had his day. In other words, if you want to continue in our employ you'll have to shut the fuck up.'

'What do you feel, Eric?' asked Sean mildly.

'I agree with Kate. I need protection – not advice.'

'But protection from who? Midas?'

'Don't be a bloody fool. Isn't it obvious? I need protection from my Auntie Liz.'

An hour later, Sean stood by the window of his room waiting for Midas to arrive. It was just after eleven and they were late. Because of the wait Eric had become increasingly agitated while Kate remained calm and detached.

The reaction to Julio's death amongst the staff of the Mas Coral had been devastating and many had wept openly. Sean had noticed that Eric had done all he could to commiserate, explaining the horror of what had happened, without admitting to being the intended target. He had also told them that the police would be coming and the discussion would have to be interrupted. Then he and Kate had disappeared into the meeting room.

Five minutes passed while Sean watched the early season tourists, wandering up towards the rocks in twos and threes, idly leaning on the stone parapet to gaze out over the sea that, fanned by a stiff breeze, was beginning to get even rougher.

Then he saw the minibus arrive at the door of the Mas Coral. Half a dozen men got out, most of them middle-aged, all wearing suits, accompanied by a couple of younger heavies who wore jeans and bomber jackets. Never had minders advertised themselves so prominently. Or were they regarded as status symbols, somewhere between a rather superior mobile phone and a pair of Gucci shoes?

Sean wondered why he wasn't accompanying Eric and Kate in similar style. If Midas needed protection, then surely Eric needed it a thousand times more.

A few minutes later, a small VW drove up and out of it

stepped a man in a blazer, open-neck white shirt, dark trousers and highly polished black shoes. As he glanced impatiently around him a waiter from the Mas Coral hurried out. The man handed over the keys and a tip, watching as the waiter drove the vehicle away.

Why couldn't he have parked the car himself? His VW wasn't exactly a status symbol, there were no passengers – and no minder. It was difficult to tell his nationality as he stepped towards the door of the restaurant, looking older than Sean had at first thought. His face was deeply tanned but wrinkled, so much so that he had the look of a leathery old tortoise. For a while he looked up and down the street, and then went inside.

Sean continued to watch the street. Then, as the heat increased, he began to feel so claustrophobic that he had to get out.

The door behind which the meeting was taking place was guarded by an arrogant young Spanish waiter who had already told Sean to either 'go out, or stay in your room'. Neither of the two suggestions had been particularly inviting.

What Sean needed to do was work out some strategy that would end not only in Eric and Kate's arrest, but Elizabeth's too. Possible arrests of Midas personnel, however, would be the real *coup de grâce*.

'I'm going for a walk. For the good of my health.'

'Your health is good?' the young Spaniard asked.

'For the moment at least.' Unlike Julio's, he thought, and then regretted the flippancy. But death had become so familiar.

The Mas Coral was closed and the blinds had been pulled down while the staff kept vigil.

Inhibited by their open grief, Sean was hurriedly making for the door when an elderly cashier placed a hand on his arm. 'We have been told you tried to save Julio. We are very grateful for your efforts.'

'I'm afraid I was too late.'

'You tried. That is enough. We want you to have a drink with us.'

'I haven't got time – '

'We won't detain you long.'

Sean hesitated. 'OK. I hope your colleagues will understand I can't stay.'

'Thank you.' He was obsequiously grateful.

The staff of the Mas Coral gazed up at Sean as he was ceremoniously led across to the central table where they sat. By the look of their shiny, slightly frayed dark suits, the elderly men had worked in the restaurant for a long time.

'This is Pele – our assistant manager.'

He was older than Julio, with a grey beard and skin which had a suety, indoor texture.

'Henri will have told you how grateful we are for trying to save the boss's life.'

'I didn't *do* anything,' Sean protested as he was handed a glass of red wine. He sipped at it, discovered how good the vintage was and took a longer swig.

'We believe we know who killed him,' said Pele. 'I have informed Mr Eric.'

Sean was instantly wary. Was this going to be a revelation, or an added complication?

'There was talk of Mr Cole being the intended victim – that the boss was in the way.'

Sean said nothing, not wanting to commit himself.

'But we know that isn't the case. There has been a feud in Estartit for a long time over the redevelopment of the harbour. Julio refused to sell out to a property company who want to build luxury apartments.'

'Surely they wouldn't assassinate him?' Then he could see that Pele didn't understand. 'What I mean is – why should they kill him? Just over a property deal?'

'Much money would have been lost if he had refused to sell.'

'He made a will, didn't he?'

'He had already made over the Mas Coral to Mr Fred.'

'Eric would have inherited then. But I'm sure he won't sell the place.'

'He already has.'

'Who to?'

'Delmar Investments own the Coral now. They are part of the

same group who want us demolished, the same group who want to build the holiday apartments.'

'But Eric's only just inherited the family business. He wouldn't have sold the restaurant – just like that.'

'Maybe he needed the capital.' Pele shrugged. 'We didn't know until we opened this morning's post.'

'Did Julio see the letter?'

'No.'

'That must rule out the property company at least.'

'We're sure it was them,' said Pele stubbornly. 'He was shot when there was no need.'

Had Eric sold the restaurant so he could raise more money for the Gatwick ring, Sean wondered. But then he realised the sale price would be nothing to the sum Midas might invest.

The phone began to ring and Henri went to the bar. After a short while he turned back to Sean. 'Señor? You have a lady calling you.'

'Hello, Sean. Isn't it a lovely day? I'm sitting out here, sunning myself.'

'Where are you, Elizabeth?' He had needed time to think. Instead he was being pulled along too fast.

'By the rocks. Where Vi made the boys swim for the patch of blue. In fact I'm looking at it now. Aren't mobile phones heaven-sent?'

'Have you heard what happened?'

'Yes, dear.'

While Elizabeth went on describing the seascape, Sean wondered whether he should report back to her, faithfully keeping to the brief she had given him – or initiate his own next move. Suppose he tried for the Triple Crown? Elizabeth, Eric, Midas. If he could break them all, his first investigation as an insider might be something of an international success.

Glancing at the beach outside, he saw a family putting up a parasol over a picnic table. A woman with two teenagers – a boy and a girl.

Sean realised that he hadn't thought about Abbie, Rik and Mary for what seemed a very long time. They and the house in Surrey belonged to another life now. Was it a life he was beginning to leave behind? Or was the healing only temporary? He suspected the latter.

Hurriedly he broke into Elizabeth's diatribe. 'You realise you got the wrong man.'

Now that she was silenced, he could hear the sound of the waves and the sudden mewing of seagulls.

'Pardon?' Elizabeth sounded bewildered. 'Surely you don't think that awful shooting had anything to do with me?'

'You mean someone else tried to beat you to it?'

'We live in a violent world.' She shrugged as if some inconvenience had occurred. 'Come down to the rocks and have a chat.'

'Can't we meet somewhere else? It's not a place of happy associations.'

'Just get down here. Like now.'

Easing the micro recorder out of his razor head, Sean taped the tiny machine under his arm and the mike to his chest. As he pulled on his shirt he wondered what would happen if it failed to work. Suppose Elizabeth made some deeply incriminating statement and he could never prove what she had said? Sean had never trusted a lap-top computer, let alone this frail-looking device.

The rocks were already swarming with sun-worshippers, although few had plucked up courage to make the scramble down to the sea, despite the fact that the wind had dropped and the surf was much less fierce. As he approached, Sean switched on the tape and hoped for the best.

Elizabeth had a light camel-hair jacket round her shoulders that was vaguely familiar. Then he remembered that Vi had worn it on their expedition to Newlands Corner.

'There's room for us both up here, Sean.' She sounded warm and friendly. Too friendly.

'You're wearing her coat.'

'It's comfy and brings back some good memories. I can still smell her lemon cologne.'

'Have you had any more thoughts about Julio's death?'

'I've already told you the business wasn't involved,' she said firmly. 'I can't understand why you should make an accusation like that. After all the trust that Vi put in your – '

'Then who?'

'Midas, of course. Eric is a fool to have anything to do with them. They'll swallow him whole.'

'And Bradman?'

'I'm sure she'll emerge triumphant. She's always struck me as a winner, not a loser like Eric.' Elizabeth spoke so viciously that Sean was surprised, not realising she was capable of such pent-up anger.

'I was told he'd sold the restaurant. Maybe he's going to sell the business too.'

'That wouldn't be so easy. Don't forget, I represent a significant group of shareholders.'

'Who don't like Eric?'

'He's consorting with the enemy, isn't he?'

'So he says.'

'Out of the horse's mouth.' Elizabeth smiled, regaining her composure. 'Would you like a peach? They're rather nice. I got them at the little shop by the harbour. I've even got a knife if you'd like me to cut one up for you.'

Sean ignored her offer. 'I thought you'd like to know I had a breakthrough after Julio's death this morning. Eric told me he was involved in the Gatwick ring.'

He had hoped to shock her, but this time she remained unruffled. 'Vi was always right.' Elizabeth thoughtfully pulled out a peach from her capacious carrier bag. 'It was only Fred who was so trusting.'

'What do you want me to do?'

'Your role has never been really clearly defined, has it? Driver. Minder. Now it looks as if you're Mr Left-Out-On-His-Ownio.'

'How about Mr Fall-Guy?'

'I don't see you that way.'

'How *do* you see me?'

'What about another role – like Mr Clever-Clogs, waiting in the wings? After all, my group of shareholders do want a result – so the time has come, the walrus said. We don't want Midas horning in, I can tell you that. They'll take us to the cleaners.'

'How much will I get paid?'

'Enough. We can discuss details like that when you've killed Eric,' she said, looking fondly out to the patch of blue.

Sean prayed the tape was working. He had a result at last, but he could hardly believe what Elizabeth had just said. He felt trapped, not just by her but by the others too.

'I'm going to ask you to repeat that.'

'You heard the first time.'

'You're acting for Vi?'

'I need to be expedient.'

'Vi and Fred didn't do murder.'

'They got done themselves.'

'I'm not a hit-man.'

'You're not really a driver or a minder either. I think Vi had the right idea about you. She saw you as a nice young man gone wrong who just wanted the right opportunity to pull himself together.'

'She hardly knew me.'

'She was perceptive, was Vi. She had a talent for it. She told me she wanted to build you up.'

'Horlicks?'

'Responsibility. Nothing like it. Between you and me I think she was wondering if you might turn out to be a bit of a son to her. Eventually I mean. Such a shame she didn't live to see that come about.'

'I only knew her for a fortnight.'

'Vi always acted on instinct. Perhaps she wanted you to have the future Andy couldn't have.' Elizabeth sounded a shade impatient. 'Well – time's ticking past, and we've got to make up our minds soon, haven't we? That meeting's not going to last for ever,' she said briskly, rummaging through her bag and bringing out a mobile phone. 'Now this is something very special.'

'What do I dial? Directory Enquiries?'

'Zero.'

'And then?'

'You'll be collected from whatever address you give.'

'Where will I be taken?'

'To a safe house.'

'And then?'

163

'When the coast is clear, as they say, you'll be returned to England. You might even do some more work for me.'

'My third owner in under a month?'

'Needs must when the devil drives. I think you should kill Kate Bradman too. Just to be on the safe side.'

'You want me to start another massacre?'

'No need to exaggerate. Midas is very bad for us both, you know. And there aren't any pills to take – except the bitter ones.'

They gazed out at the patch of blue.

'Why did Vi make the boys go in over the rocks?' asked Sean. 'It's much easier the other side.'

'She knew how tough life was going to be for them.'

'Rites of passage?'

'Just a bit of rigour. It sharpens us all up. After all, she had her share.'

'I can understand why she made Andrew do his bit of rigour, but why Eric? Did Vi hope he'd drown?'

'Of course not. She just wanted him to be a man.'

'*Her* man?'

'You're a canny sort of bloke, aren't you?'

'Suppose your mobile lets me down?'

'Trust me.' She got up, stumbling slightly, but she didn't remind him of Vi's vulnerability. Elizabeth suddenly seemed immensely strong. 'I must get a taxi to the airport. We don't want to be seen together, do we?'

'That's what you said at the funeral.'

'Give it your best shot.'

'Don't you mean shots?'

'And you'll be rewarded.' She reached into her bag and dragged out a small parcel. 'You'd better have this. Unless you've got a nice little shooter already.'

'I lost mine.'

'Don't keep telling me what a good little minder you are.'

'There's something else.'

'Be quick or I'll turn into a pumpkin.'

'Suppose Midas have got a contract out on him already.'

'I don't think there's much doubt about that.'

'Then what the hell do you want *me* to kill Eric for?'

'I always enjoy a competition, don't you? Especially against such a worthy opponent. You could be a giant killer, Sean. Go for Eric first. Vi would have wanted that. And of course Kate's the jam in the doughnut.'

Sean walked slowly back to the restaurant, for the second time that day. His first reaction had been shock, then incredulity and then shock again. It was as if he was a juggler, keeping so many balls in the air. His focus had to be total, despite the fact that he was sure he was going to fail. But if he *could* keep the balls going, he knew he could win.

Hurrying on, suddenly unable to take the full weight of responsibility, Sean contemplated getting drunk in his room. Both warring sides were depending on his obedience. But which one was setting him up?

He stopped at a stand and bought himself a large greasy-looking hamburger. The sides of the slightly stale bun oozed oil and mayonnaise while the meat was tough and unidentifiable. Dead meat.

With sudden ferocity Sean hurled the hamburger into the gutter where it was pursued by a mangy dog and a screaming gull. The dog won.

As Sean headed back to the Mas Coral, a woman approached him. She was young and attractive and angry.

'Are you English?'

'Are you?' He tried to push past but she was standing solidly in his way.

'Yes – as it happens.'

'What do you do? Try and spot fellow Brits?'

'If they throw rubbish around I do.'

'It's been eaten.'

'Not the wrapping.'

'The dog didn't fancy that.'

'I'm serious. I happen to live here.'

'On the street? You do business here? I didn't realise you were on the game. Sorry I haven't got enough small change on me.' Sean was enjoying his mockery.

'So you're an insulting yob too.'

'I do my best.'

'I'm sick to death of British tourists letting us down.'

'You been stood up?'

The woman turned abruptly away from him. 'I can't take any more of this.' Her voice shook and Sean was immediately repentant.

'I'm sorry.'

'What?'

He bent down and picked up the greasy wrapper, sticking it into the pocket of his jeans.

'I'm sorry.'

She looked at him in amazement and her eyes filled with tears.

'I haven't always been like this,' he said. 'I've just sort of grown into it.'

'Señor Pollard? Emilio Rodriguez. Barcelona police.'

He was standing outside the Mas Coral in the late morning heat, wearing a dark suit with a formal tie and a crumpled shirt.

'I want to talk to you about Julio Puig's murder.'

'Where's Mr Cole?'

'He's gone back to his meeting. There is a place where we can talk privately. I'll take you there.'

Estartit Nautique was a showroom on the harbour packed with high-powered speedboats, outboard engines, designer wetsuits and a gleaming display of technical accessories every discerning yachts-person should have aboard their sailing boat or floating gin palace.

Rodriguez nodded to a young man at a desk and led the way up a flight of steps to the first floor where behind stacked boxes of spare parts was a small and grubby office with a state of the art Gaggia coffee machine.

'Would you like a café Americano?'

'Thank you.'

'And a Cognac?' He went to a cupboard, brought out a half-empty bottle and poured the brandy into glasses and the coffee into large, white cups. 'Please, sit down.'

There were two chairs, one each side of a small table, and as Sean faced Rodriguez he wondered how long the interview was going to last. Was the meeting at the Mas Coral over? Would

Eric be angry and suspicious? Above all, would he still have time to think over Elizabeth's extraordinary proposition?

'I hope you are pleased to see me,' said Rodriguez with unexpected self-effacement.

Sean gazed at him curiously.

'Particularly when I tell you that I represent Señor Farringdon.'

Thank God, he thought. Contact at last.

Sean placed the micro tape on the table, praying it would work. He pressed the start button, and after what seemed an interminable delay Elizabeth's voice came over in satisfying clarity. 'There's room for us both up here.'

Rodriguez took notes as the taped conversation continued in all its candour.

'I congratulate you,' he said eventually as he switched off. 'When did she leave for the airport?'

'She got a taxi about twenty minutes ago. You going to stop her?'

'I hope so.'

'And then?'

'I can assume you will not be carrying out her instructions, despite your loss of income?'

'Perhaps Señor Farringdon will be able to reimburse me.'

'Perhaps. Can you explain Señor Cole's involvement in this?'

'He told me he operated a drug-running ring based at Gatwick airport with Bradman and they have come to Estartit to negotiate a Midas investment.'

'We've been trying to expose Midas for a long time. Maybe we have a chance now.'

'I'm also pretty certain they killed the Coles and the Corsinis.'

'And Julio Puig?'

'Eric must have been the target. Julio got in the way.'

'Does Eric trust you?'

'I think so.'

'What about his relationship with Bradman?'

'It's more the other way round. I think she's had him in her sights for quite a while. Or rather in Midas's sights.'

'Do they have a sexual relationship?'

167

'Unsatisfactory. She recently discovered Eric was bisexual.'

'I'm sorry that I have to ask this. Has he propositioned you?'

'Nothing specific. But it's there.'

'Why are you so sure he's telling the truth about his involvement in this Gatwick ring?'

'I didn't say I was. But I do have some reason to believe him.'

'Why?' Rodriguez looked sceptical.

'I got into a bit of a scrape.' Sean didn't want to tell him about the night by the weir. An admission to attempted suicide hardly made him the most stable of insiders.

'A scrape? What does that mean?'

'I almost fell into a river. Eric saved my life.'

'For a purpose.' Rodriguez got up. 'There is something we found out that might be useful. You were all three booked to fly out tomorrow from Girona but there was a problem about the plane and Señor Cole changed his schedule.'

'What kind of problem?'

'Apparently a small repair had to be made to some overhead luggage compartments and the aircraft had to be taken out of service. Cole reserved three seats on another flight, but the original aircraft was fixed more rapidly than expected and put back into service. Curiously, Mr Cole changed his schedule again.'

'The implication being . . .'

'That the heroin is on board.'

'So why should Eric need to travel with the stuff? He doesn't have to hold anyone's hand, does he?'

'In my opinion, he won't be travelling anywhere.'

'Midas won't let him?'

'Neither will Bradman. I can't understand why he hasn't got you with him.'

'That's because he trusts Bradman. But I think he's worried about the return journey.'

'Are you armed?'

'Not by him.'

'What does that mean?'

Sean gave him Elizabeth's packet. 'Valuable evidence of evil intent.' he said. 'Can you look after it?'

'I should be delighted. You've done well.' Rodriguez paused. I have this strong feeling the balloon is about to go up. Isn't that what the British used to say in the Second World War? What does it mean exactly?'

'I'm not really sure,' said Sean. 'But it was never a happy event.'

19

The phone rang. As Rodriguez picked it up, Sean felt more confident than he had ever done since he had first driven for Vi and the whole bizarre affair had begun.

He knew he was witnessing a collapsing dynasty being dragged into the open maw that was Midas – but with luck he could damage them too.

As Rodriguez put the phone down with a smile of satisfaction, Sean's new-found optimism soared even higher.

'We got her. She was coming out of the Hertz office at Girona.'

'She has an associate there. But she's not worth bothering about. Where's Elizabeth now?'

'On the way here.'

'Why here?'

'I want to see if you can get any more information out of her. You might be a little more threatening than I.'

'And then?'

'She'll be detained in Barcelona.'

'I'll need to contact Eric. I don't want to foul up now.'

'Why don't you call the restaurant.'

'This is Pollard. Is Mr Cole still in the meeting?'

'Yes, Señor.'

'Say I'm taking a walk and I'll be back at eight.'

'I'll see to it that he gets the message.'

Sean put down the phone. 'I have to make that deadline.'

'It's only four. I think we have plenty of time for our show-down.' Rodriguez seemed increasingly fond of his English colloquialisms.

When Elizabeth arrived, escorted by a police officer, Sean had rarely seen such control. There was no denial, no outrage, just a

170

bewilderment that was almost convincing. She came across as an Englishwoman, not used to travelling abroad, a bit rough and ready but ordinary enough, far too ordinary to be mixed up in anything like this.

She still wore Vi's jacket over her immaculately cut black trousers, but her long blonde hair was tousled as if she had run her hands through it and there was a dark smudge under her right eye.

The police officer left and Rodriguez brought in another chair for himself. As Sean sat down behind the desk facing her, Elizabeth lit up a cigarette, scattering ash on the floor, and they made uneasy eye contact. He was the first to look away.

'Have you been told I'm an undercover police officer and I taped our conversation on the rocks?'

'It wasn't a very kind thing to do, was it, Sean?'

'Would you like me to play you the tape?'

'That won't be necessary. I know exactly what I said.' Her voice shook just a little.

'You offered me a large sum of money to kill Eric Cole and Kate Bradman.'

'You silly boy. Why did you take an old woman so seriously?'

Rodriguez laid the automatic on the table between them. 'I think this is serious enough, isn't it?'

'I was rather hoping you'd come clean and *tell* me you were a policeman.'

Sean gazed at her incredulously as his confidence suddenly drained. So did Rodriguez.

'You tried to establish my identity by proposing a contract killing? What did you expect me to say? I happen to be an officer of the law, madam, and I can't commit murder by proxy?'

'You didn't ring true. There was something wrong. I'm sure Eric feels the same.'

'So why hasn't he sussed me out?'

'You ought to have seen him as a kid. He could spin out those games of his for days at a time.'

Suppose – just suppose – she was telling the truth? But if Eric had guessed, then why *was* he stringing him along?

'I still don't understand why you should offer me a contract killing.'

171

Elizabeth sighed wearily. 'I needed to prove you were an undercover agent, Mr Pollard. If nothing happened to Eric and Kate then that would seem to be the proof I needed.'

'And if something *did* happen to them?'

'It would have been entirely your responsibility. But I expect Midas will have moved in by now.'

'That wasn't Eric's intention.'

'More like Kate's. I'm sure that little bitch has worked a flanker on us all.'

Sean was amazed at Elizabeth's ability to be so inventive.

'Do you admit that Vi and Fred Cole's business is a criminal organisation?' asked Rodriguez quietly.

'They dealt in property.'

'How long were you a partner?'

'I never was a partner. I was Vi's friend and I had a few shares. When she died I was approached by the anti-Eric brigade, and I can assure you there are an awful lot of them. They just needed some leadership, that's all. I always was a business woman.'

'Tell me how it was run.'

'A board with a managing director. Or rather two in this case. Vi and Fred.'

'When I was living at St Tropez,' said Sean, 'I found it very strange that Vi was so isolated. She never went to a meeting. No one ever came to the house. The business seemed to run itself.'

'How long were you there?' Elizabeth asked mockingly.

'A fortnight.'

'Far too short a time to make judgements like that.'

'I don't think so. I know the business was just a front for criminal activities which were organised into self-operating units. Vi was redundant. She had a lot of time on her hands.'

'Absolute nonsense.' Elizabeth turned to Rodriguez, 'Do we have to go on with all this crap?' For some reason she now sounded intensely irritated.

'You must co-operate with us. There is incriminating information on the tape – '

'I insist on having a lawyer.'

'I'm having you held in Barcelona until further arrests have been made.'

'You know you don't have enough evidence,' scoffed Elizabeth, but she was beginning to sound uneasy.

'I think we do,' said Sean. 'But Eric can always provide some more if necessary.'

'He'd never tell you anything. You didn't fool him for a minute,' she said scornfully, but he could see he had unsettled her and capitalised on it.

'Eric enjoys playing games with me.' He explained what had happened the evening before Roberto and Maria were murdered and noted with satisfaction that he had succeeded in alarming her yet again.

Elizabeth clearly felt the need to explain. 'He used to live in a world of his own as a child. It seemed harmless enough. But now you've told me what happened at St Tropez, I'm not particularly surprised. Eric needed to fantasise. I wish I could.'

'You'd known Vi all your life?'

'We were brought up together. We both lived in the same street in Clapham and our mothers were good mates. Vi and I were both only children and over the years, what with going to the same school, seeing each other every day, playing together, we got to be more like sisters than friends. She married. I didn't. She had kids. I never had kids. But I wasn't jealous and none of that ever made a difference.'

Sean was sure that Elizabeth was lying. 'And yet, all the time I was at Vi's, she never mentioned your name.'

'She didn't want me to come over. Not with her new minder around.'

She was back on the defensive now.

'That doesn't ring true, Elizabeth. Like I didn't ring true to you. So what's the real reason?'

'I remember a time when Vi and I were taking a bit of sun down on the beach at Margate,' she said reminiscently, avoiding his question. 'Eric was seven and Andrew couldn't have been more than five. The tide was out and Eric had built this castle. Well, it was more than that – a walled city really – and he'd moulded the whole thing out of wet sand. Amazing sight. Bit like the Spanish bloke who put up that cathedral in Barcelona . . .'

'Gaudi,' Rodriguez prompted.

'You've never seen anything like it. Anyway, along comes young Andy. Well, he wasn't to know, was he?'

'Wasn't to know what?' Sean had decided to let her think the red herring was working.

'That the city really meant something to Eric. I can see it now. His world, the one he'd built for himself, not the real one where there wasn't any love. Anyway, it wasn't really Andy's fault, he was only a babe, so he comes and clobbers the whole bloody lot.'

'What did Eric do?'

'He just stood and watched and listened.'

'Listened to what?'

'To Vi laughing, of course.'

'Didn't she realise what the sand city meant to Eric?'

'Of course she did.'

'Then why laugh?'

'She wanted to hurt him, didn't she?'

'Did she hate him that much? He was only a child – '

'Vi loved Fred. He went with other women and she knew it, but what she didn't want to see was the living evidence.'

'Did *you* ever sleep with Fred?' asked Sean suddenly.

'No way.'

'So *you* wouldn't be Eric's mother then?'

For a moment Elizabeth seemed completely thrown. There was also a fleeting expression of fear in her eyes. Then Sean wondered if he might have imagined it.

Someone revved up an outboard engine in the shop below so noisily that they all avoided each other's gaze until the juddering roar stopped as unexpectedly as it had started.

'No,' she said quietly. 'I'm not.'

Sean allowed a silence to develop. Soon it seemed as deafening as the outboard.

'Did Vi ever suspect you were?'

'Of course she didn't.'

'Was that the reason she wouldn't see you?'

'You're talking rubbish.'

'Am I? Suppose someone had told her?'

174

She didn't reply.

'Let me ask you another question, Elizabeth. If you were such a close friend of Vi's – almost like sisters, as you said – why were you left out of the funeral arrangements?'

'I don't know.'

'You must.'

She was struggling for control again. 'I was hurt – you could see that.'

'If you really are Eric's mother, it can easily be proved. Medically, I mean.'

'I know that.'

'What you don't know is that we could enforce a test.' Sean glanced at Rodriguez, hoping he would back up the bluff.

'Of course we can do this.'

'You've no right,' She was getting flustered.

'We have every right,' said Rodriguez. 'This is a criminal investigation.'

'For Christ's sake. What's all this got to do with an investigation?' She was confused now.

'Come on.' Sean was insistent. 'You need to tell us.'

'I don't *need* to tell you anything.' She paused, letting another silence develop. Then she said, 'So what if I am his mother?'

Sean breathed a sigh of relief. 'Does he know?'

'Absolutely not.'

'What about Vi?'

'I took great care she was never told.'

'So how did she find out?'

'I don't know.'

'You must have some idea.'

'She went overboard on you, dear. Didn't she?'

'What's that got to do with it?'

'In my opinion it was compensatory.'

'*Who* told her?' Sean shouted, needing to shatter the last shreds of evasion.

'I have this feeling that Fred had dropped a hint.'

'Why should he?'

'Bit of conscience? Anyway – she told me to piss off. So I did.'

'I just can't understand why Fred should have told Vi anything at all, not after all this time. I mean that kind of confession wasn't going to help his case.'

'All right.' Elizabeth got up. 'I told her, didn't I? And the reason I did it was to make her fight harder against that clause in the will.'

'You sacrificed your friendship with Vi for that?' So that's why she'd been pissed in the afternoons.

'Frankly I've grown to hate the bastard.'

'The bastard's your son.'

'He was an accident.'

'So Vi didn't leave you any money?'

'Not a bean.'

'Why did you say she had?'

'Sounded better.'

'But you are working for the business?'

'They know how much I can hate.'

'Didn't you want to protect Eric when he was young?'

'I knew I didn't have a chance.'

'You were Vi's closest friend.' Sean was trying to make Elizabeth lose her temper. 'So why *did* you cheat on her?'

'Fred and I were drunk. It was a one-night stand.'

'Why didn't you have an abortion?'

'I wanted the child. At the time. There didn't seem much chance of having another.'

'There's more to it than that, isn't there?' If there was, why should she tell him? She had sacrificed Eric and she certainly wouldn't hesitate to do so again. 'Was Fred going to divorce Vi? Bring you into the business in her place?'

'At one point I thought he would, but in the end he gave me some shares and that was my lot. Vi thought he was being generous because I was always so broke.'

'So how did you come to hate Eric?'

'It wasn't difficult. He left me behind. I've been a hairdresser all my life but I've never had a bean. Eventually I managed to get a couple of shops off the ground but a few months later I went bust. OK, maybe it was my own fault.'

'What happened next?'

'Eric sent me a cheque. It was a large one and I knew where he'd got the money from. Those drugs. I wasn't going to accept it. No way.'

'But you did.'

'It kept me going.'

'Suppose Midas kills him? Won't you give a toss?'

Elizabeth didn't reply.

Rodriguez got to his feet, impatient now. 'You'll not be allowed visitors for the next few days. We don't want Señor Pollard's cover blown.'

'You can't do that.'

'We can,' said Rodriguez.

'There's no charge.'

'How about incitement to murder?' suggested Sean. 'That might do for a start.'

The meeting was still continuing on the first floor of the shuttered Mas Coral as Sean returned. He had watched Elizabeth being taken away in Rodriguez's car and had almost felt sorry for her. It was as if she had taken illicit bites out of someone's apple and had found out too late the fruit was poisoned.

'Your health is good?' asked the young Spaniard, now more than a little martyred as he sat on a hard-backed chair.

'Never better,' he replied, taking care to slam the bedroom door in his face.

Sean drank some tepid mineral water and then lay on the hard bed, trying to view each of his conspirators in a more perceptive light.

How much had Vi known? Had she really been so prejudiced against Eric when he was young? Did she really not know who his mother was until Elizabeth had told her? It seemed unlikely – but just possible.

Fred was almost an unknown quantity. It was true that he had been powerful – but how powerful? Who were his associates and had Elizabeth been one of them? Was Eric really her child? He wouldn't put it past her to have made it all up.

Eric was the most complex of them all, playing games to survive emotionally, as shadowy as his dead brother, still immersed in a labyrinth of his own making. But surely his outright rejection by Vi accounted for all that? Playing games at home was one thing though. With Midas, another.

Elizabeth's role in the Coles' lives had begun with dependence and ended in bitter loathing. More significantly, she had nothing to lose.

Finally, there was Kate who must have targeted her victim a long time ago, and Eric's only unwitting revenge had been his sexual inadequacy. Sean suddenly realised that although he knew what she looked like, he knew nothing more about her.

The knock was soft and hesitant and Sean got up slowly, his head reeling with unanswered questions, mainly about Kate.

When he opened the door he had never seen Eric looking so defeated.

'Where's your girlfriend?'

'In bed with a headache. Would you like to go for a drink?'

'What about the meeting?'

'The police interrupted several times and I had to endure a couple of interrogations, but at least we're going to be allowed to fly back tomorrow.'

'And what about Midas?'

Eric didn't answer immediately. Then he said carefully, 'I've made a bit of a financial killing. I've been bought out.'

'You mean they've taken everything?' Sean hoped he sounded suitably surprised.

'The business. And Gatwick too. They're relieving me of a number of onerous responsibilities.'

'What's Kate's view?'

'I don't know. She seems played out.' His unintentional use of the word was ironic. 'So we're going for the twelve o'clock flight.' Eric came in and closed the door. 'I've got a little present for you.'

'Where did you get it?'

'I made the arrangements last night.'

'Am I going to need it?'

'You might.'

'I thought you said your problems were over – that they'd all been taken off your hands. So what are you afraid of?'

'Don't fuck with me. Not now.'

'What's the problem?'

Eric suddenly decided to come clean 'There's heroin stashed in some false sections in the overhead lockers. Our people will deal with the recovery, but I'm going to need you to be vigilant on the way to the airport – and on the way back home.'

'Do you really think you're at risk?'

'I might be offering you a permanent protection job.'

'I'm not sure I want it.'

Eric took the small automatic from his pocket and gave it to Sean. At least he hadn't gift-wrapped it, like Elizabeth.

'How did you manage the flight rescheduling?'

'We have someone in air traffic control.'

'And they're now working for Midas?'

'I don't give a sod. Gatwick was never my party.'

'Whose was it then?'

'Andrew's.'

Sean thanked God that Vi had never known. He was also surprised that he cared so much.

'Don't you believe me?' asked Eric flatly.

'You'd better explain.' Sean wondered whether he had arrived at the centre of the labyrinth or not.

'Andrew and Kate were partners, but I don't think he ever really trusted her – particularly when he found out about the Midas connection. That's why he brought me in. But the time wasn't right for a takeover then. The ring wasn't big enough.'

'You made it grow?'

'And now it'll grow some more.'

'Did you ever think Midas would swallow you?'

'Kate assured me they wouldn't.'

'You trusted her?'

'It was a mistake.'

'How have they paid you?'

'Banker's draft on an offshore account. I don't see it bouncing. It's me who might do that – unless I can rely on you.'

Sean knew that he had to keep sober as Eric led him into a network of cheap night-clubs in Estartit, crammed with drunken holiday-makers imbibing lager in plastic glasses. As they trailed from bar to bar Eric became increasingly depressed and Sean realised that he was going to have a difficult evening.

'What the fuck's the matter with you?' Eric complained as he ordered another large brandy and half a lager. 'Why don't you have a chaser or something?'

'I'm not a drinker.'

'I hadn't noticed that before. What about that evening when you tried to top yourself?'

'That was different.'

'Relax.'

'I am.'

'With a chaser.'

'No way.'

'Why do you want to stay sober?'

'I told you – I want to relax. To unwind. I can't do that if I'm pissed.'

'I can,' Eric replied. 'All too easily.'

'I'm sorry you've been taken to the cleaners. But at least you've made a bomb out of it.'

'That's an unfortunate way of putting it.'

'Unfortunate maybe, but true.'

'I was a fucking idiot, right out of my depth. I really thought Kate would act in my interests, but she and Midas had obviously planned this rip-off for a long time.'

'Why did the meeting take so long?'

'Because I tried to negotiate. But I soon realised I wasn't exactly in a negotiating position.'

'Has Kate always worked for Midas?'

'She sees projects through for them.'

'What's her background?'

'High-flyer. Daddy's in oil. Mummy's got a shop in Fulham. Lampshades, I think. But Kate's always been a head-hunter.'

'You never saw through that?'

'I was too arrogant. Too anxious to impress her.'

'Was Andrew's death accidental? Or was he pushed?'

'He was already addicted.'

'Would Kate agree with you?'

'Yes.' He wasn't defensive, just puzzled, and Sean had the sudden conviction that Eric was telling the truth. 'Gatwick was just ripe for the picking and ready to harvest. Just like dear old Dad and Mum. I was a fool to trust Kate and I was a fool to trust you. She led me by the fucking nose, but you're a wild card. A real problem to a player.'

'But you still want me to protect you.'

'I don't have another candidate, do I?'

Sean was beginning to wonder why Eric was so low key. Why wasn't he slagging Kate off? Then he wondered if, after all, Eric was prepared to take the money and run. But he'd have to run hard.

'I need you, Sean. Much more than I need Kate.'

With a deadening certainty Sean knew that Eric would come in as useful bait for Midas, providing he was able to keep him alive, and Farringdon certainly wouldn't allow him to let go for the foreseeable future. It was a depressing thought. Sean decided to go on pushing, anxious to find out what Eric might blurt out when drunk.

'Kate seems a little restless.'

'What the fuck are you trying to say?'

'She thinks you fancy me.' Sean delivered the blow equably.

'Is that what she's been telling you?' Eric was suitably stung.

'We can't talk in here.' The disco beat was softer now and some of the drinkers were already looking curiously in their direction.

'I need another drink.'

'Get some brandy. We'll go outside.'

He watched Eric Cole stumble towards the bar, trying to make his way in a world that wasn't made of sand. Sean knew he now had the chance to really manipulate him while he was at his most humiliated.

They sat on an upturned dinghy, looking out at the islands as security lights roved amongst the rocks. Now the Medas seemed threatening, dominating Estartit like Eric's sand city might have dominated Andrew.

Out here, in the windless Mediterranean night, Eric seemed resigned and full of drunken self-pity.

'So Kate told you I was no good in bed. Just like my poor old mum.'

'Maybe she felt threatened.'

'Why the hell did she tell you all this?' demanded Eric.

'I told you. Because she thought I might be your lover.'

'Christ!'

'What's odd about that? After all, you hired me.'

'She seems to have misunderstood the reason.'

'Did she?'

'There was more to it than that.'

'Was there?' Suddenly Sean's adrenalin was pumping.

'I did fancy you – '

'You put the "fancy" in the past.'

'But I fancied Kate more.'

'Because she had a thing going with Andrew?'

'You're a perceptive git, aren't you? That's what my mother might have liked about you.' Eric paused. 'You're right. I wanted what he'd got.'

'And Vi? Wasn't she the only girl for you?'

'Oddly enough, I found her death a release.'

'How close were you to Elizabeth?'

'Not particularly. When we were kids she was always Mum's lieutenant, but recently they seemed to fall out. I think she had something going with Dad. But what does it matter? It was inevitable. Like I told you, Mum was no good in bed. Just like me.'

'You said you were relieved when she died. Had you stopped loving her?'

'I didn't think so.' Eric poured more brandy into the two glasses he'd stolen from the bar. 'Do you ever read?' he asked patronisingly.

'Only if there aren't too many difficult words.'

'There was a Somerset Maugham story where this young thief sat in his cell for two years thinking about his lover all day every day. He'd gone inside deeply in love, but when he came out he suddenly realised he couldn't stand the sight of her.'

'And that was the same with your mother?'

'She dominated my life. I thought about her every day. In the end I burnt out.'

'Didn't you grieve?'

'Not like I thought I would.'

'What about your birth mother? Do you ever think of her?'

'No.' Eric looked surprised.

'You made no attempt to find her?'

'Why should I with Vi around? She made all mothers a bad joke.'

'And now?'

'I feel nothing for either of them.'

'So what about the future?'

'I'll be glad to get away.'

'Where?'

'God knows. I rather fancied travelling for a while. A companion would be fun. Maybe you'd consider joining me? I'd be your sugar daddy.'

'You sound like one of those intrepid Edwardian lady travellers who always had paid companions. Rose Macaulay, for instance.'

'I didn't realise you were so well read.'

The comment was innocent enough but it made Sean come to a grinding halt, almost drying up completely, irrevocably becoming Danny again. Abbie also read Rose Macaulay and they had discussed her avidly. Had the brandy lured him into lowering his guard? Tongue-tied like an awkward child, he gazed at Eric blankly, unable to finish his sentence, unable to play Sean any longer. It was a terrible feeling. Danny was back, eating Sean alive.

'What's the matter?'

'I forgot what I was going to say.'

'There's something about you that's always on the edge, isn't there, Sean? A real cliff-hanger. Sometimes I think you're a bit of a Kate Bradman yourself. So who the fuck are you?'

'I thought I was in the clear. That you'd sussed me out at last.'

'Who are you, Sean?' Eric repeated.

'I'm a main-chancer.'

'You're more than that. You're like one of those worms you find in the tropics – the kind that slips into your ear and works its way down inside your body. You're an infestation.'

Eric got up and stood before him, glass in hand, swaying

slightly, and Sean realised with relief that he was drunker than he had imagined. Once the realisation was complete, Danny receded.

'What are you? Just a fucking infestation, that's all.'

Eric drank deeply and then over-cautiously put his glass down by the side of the boat and stood the empty brandy bottle on the pebbles.

'Time for all God-fearing little boys to go to bed. So why don't you get a life?'

Sean wished to God he could.

20

'I'm going for a walk,' Eric had told Sean, and he had known better than to interfere.

Now, as Sean returned to the Mas Coral, he saw the restaurant was in darkness. The side door, however, was open and he could make out a figure sitting at the bar. There was no one else around.

'Kate?'

'Where's Eric?'

'In the town.'

'Pissed?'

'Something like that. Are you?'

'No.' She held up a glass of orange juice.

'You're sitting up for him?'

'No chance. We're finished.'

'So is the business, I gather.'

'It's been taken over.'

'That's what I mean,' said Sean. 'Isn't anyone going to lock up?'

'I've got the keys.'

'They're very trusting.'

'I'm not taking them over too. I've arranged to have the restaurant sold back to the staff – as a mark of respect for Julio.'

'How wonderful it must be to have that kind of power.'

'I'm not exactly amongst the great and the good.'

'So why did you target Eric?'

'Obvious reasons.'

'Harvesting? Another acquisition for Midas?'

'Something like that.'

'So the business was worth having.'

'It was my last bow.'

Sean sat down beside her. 'What's that meant to mean?'

'I had this call.'

'Yes?'

'Midas are letting me go.'

'Why?'

185

'I've been with them a long time. Maybe they don't think I'm as good as I was – that I don't bring in the juicy acquisitions any longer, that I'm not up to scratch.'

'How does that leave you? I mean – you know so much about Midas. You could blow them wide open.'

'Midas doesn't really let anyone go.'

'You mean they'll kill you too?'

'Maybe not immediately.'

'And Eric?'

She nodded.

'Can't you get some protection?'

'It's not worth it.'

'So what are you going to do? Sit and wait for it to happen?'

'Not a chance.' Kate smiled. 'I've been expecting this, I suppose. I guessed they thought I might be tired. So I've already made some plans.'

'But you're not going to tell me about them.'

'Got it in one.'

'So why tell me half the story?'

'Got to talk to someone.'

'What made you do it in the first place?' said Sean curiously.

'I was always a clever girl at networking. That's what it's all about. That's what it's always been about. You can get addicted. Badly.'

'And there's no detox?'

'It's not worth it. Not if there's no future.'

Sean took her hand but she pulled it away.

'I don't want it now. I've got too much to think about.'

'Can't I help? You need to switch off.'

'That's the last thing I can afford to do,' Kate said. 'One of these days we'll all go down together,' she added obliquely.

'What's that meant to mean?'

'You'll see.'

Next morning, Sean drove Kate and Eric away from Estartit. The Medas Islands were just breaking through the early morning mist, primeval and beautiful, a world apart from the empty lager cans, plastic glasses, hamburger wrappers, condoms and other human debris that littered the streets. Sean had a mental image

186

of Fred Cole mooring his boat off the islands and then remembered how Kate had wanted to get permission to land.

'Those islands,' he muttered. 'They're incredible.'

'Only for the lonely,' said Eric vacuously.

But Kate seemed to take him at his word. 'I'd give a lot to be lonely.' She took a last look at the islands as they turned the corner, taking the road to Girona.

Sean drove towards the *autopista*, checking the traffic behind him. The morning was intensely hot and as he put on the air-conditioning, he caught a glimpse of Eric and Kate's grey, exhausted faces in the mirror.

'I don't want to bring up any more problems, but how do you propose to get my little shooter through security?'

'Leave it to me,' Kate replied with a mysterious confidence.

Sean was just about to press her on the subject when Eric snapped, 'Wait a minute.' He was gazing into the wing mirror. 'Why doesn't he overtake? Can't you lose him?'

Then Sean saw the motorcycle despatch rider too. He was just behind them.

'I could try, but I'd rather wait till we're on the motorway.'

'Suppose he comes alongside?' asked Kate uneasily.

'The road's too narrow. Can't you see that bloody great ditch on either side? He's not likely to try anything here.'

'What about the toll booths?'

'Let Sean make the decision,' said Eric. 'I'm sure he's capable. After all, that's why we hired him.'

The motorbike still remained at a distance, even when he slowed down on a wider section of the road, but as they went through the toll he accelerated, disappearing from sight.

After a couple more kilometres, however, the despatch rider reappeared, still making no attempt to overtake.

'Maybe the guy just isn't in a hurry,' suggested Eric.

Sean accelerated enough to leave the bike in the distance, and after another five minutes returned to the middle lane, checking his mirror carefully.

'I don't see him now,' he said.

'He could have been trying to contact us,' suggested Eric. 'Maybe Midas want to apologise.'

'Your sense of humour always does grate,' said Kate.

'You sold us out.'

'Surely we've discussed the problem enough.'

'We've hardly begun.'

They were squabbling in front of him as if he wasn't there again, and Sean hoped the good and faithful servant might have his chance to divide and rule.

Eric glanced at his watch. 'We'll be at the airport in an hour. I'm sure it's going to be all right.'

'I don't trust your judgement.'

'My, we *are* a doubting Thomasina.'

'Why don't you keep your camp jokes to yourself?'

'You led me into the lions' den, Kate,' Eric reminded her again. 'You're lucky I'm still prepared to joke at all.'

'You've made a fortune.'

'But for how long?'

It was only then that Sean realised Kate and Eric weren't really divided at all. They were united – in fear.

'Here he comes again.'

'Christ!' Kate was getting agitated but Eric seemed to have more of a grip.

'I'm going into that service area,' said Sean. 'I don't want him to try anything on the motorway.'

'That's a bad move,' began Eric.

'We're not playing games,' snapped Kate.

'Not any more.' Sean pulled over at the last moment, the Punto's tyres screaming as he swung the wheel.

'I have to tell you he's still following us,' said Eric with almost smug satisfaction.

As they pulled up at the pumps, the tension mounted.

'For Christ's sake, don't let us down this time.' Eric had slumped down in his seat, keeping well away from the window, all too aware that the despatch rider had now pulled in right behind them.

Sean was suddenly reminded of the moments before the bomb exploded at St Tropez. Familiar objects stood out in stark relief. The pumps, the canopies, the shop, the advertisements – they all seemed sinister, significant.

The motorbike was glinting in the hard sunlight and he checked the automatic in his jacket pocket. Slowly Sean opened the door and as casually as he could manage strolled over to the pump, picked up the nozzle and flipped open the Punto's petrol cap, unlocking it with the ignition key.

The despatch rider was in his early twenties and dressed in heavy biker gear. As he dismounted and began to walk briskly towards the Punto, all Sean's worst fears were realised.

'Get down on the floor and wind up that fucking window fast. Both of you.'

Kate and Eric clumsily obeyed him, crowding each other, only concerned with their own self-preservation.

The despatch rider was short and wiry with a thin, clean-shaven face. He was pale and the Mediterranean sun had yet to reach him.

'What's that you said?' he asked in a South London whine.

'I was talking to my passengers.'

'Sorry to bother you.'

'Did you want something?'

The young man gazed into the Punto and laughed spontaneously, genuinely amused. 'Quite an item, aren't they?'

Sean took out the petrol nozzle and replaced it with a steely clang.

'What do you want?'

He shrugged. 'Look – I just need to – '

Sean grabbed him, twisting his arm up behind his back and forcing his head on to the bonnet of the Punto. Fortunately there were no other vehicles nearby. He wanted to hurt their pursuer, hurt him badly.

'Jesus Christ!'

'Who are you?'

'Brennan. Patrick Brennan.'

'What do you want?' Sean forced his arm further up his back. 'You were following us.'

'I recognised one of your passengers and I wanted to speak to him, for Christ's sake. Now will you let me go?'

Sean released Brennan's arm and he stood up, tears of pain in his eyes.

'Get your hands above your head.'

'What for?'

'I'm going to frisk you.'

Painfully, Brennan obeyed, but after a careful search Sean found nothing.

'There was no need for that,' he muttered.

'Why did you follow us?' Sean felt a sense of heady triumph.

'You deaf or something?'

'You want to go back on that bonnet?'

Brennan backed away, rubbing at his arm, looking partly outraged, partly afraid. 'That guy owes me money.'

'Who?'

'The one in the back who's lying on the floor with the lady on top. He owes me.'

Sean gazed at Brennan, completely baffled, wondering whether this was some kind of trick. 'What for?'

'Services rendered.'

'What do you mean?'

'He was a bit the worse for wear but I let him have what he wanted and he didn't pay me. I decided to hang around the Mas Coral this morning. Good thing I did.'

'How much does he owe you?'

'Hundred and fifty.'

Sean tapped on the car window and Kate and Eric gazed up, still huddled together. He had difficulty in suppressing a grin.

'This gentleman *does* want to make contact, but he hasn't come from where you thought he'd come. I believe he's one of your more private creditors.'

'I don't understand.' But Eric was already sweating profusely, looking as if he was unlikely to ever leave the floor of the Punto.

Kate levered herself up to the seat, kicking him, shuddering slightly as if the contact had made her feel unclean. 'You prick!'

Eric got up and dragged out his wallet, counting the notes, passing over a hundred.

'That's not enough.'

Sean was looking at his watch. They still had time to catch the flight but the delay was turning into a disturbing farce.

'You still owe me another fifty.'

190

Without comment, Eric passed another wad through the window.

'You ran a stupid risk following us like that,' said Sean. 'I could have called the police on my mobile.'

'You have to take risks in this game or you get ripped off. You his girlfriend?' Brennan asked Kate.

'On your way,' said Sean aggressively, the heady sense of power returning.

'OK.' He strolled back to his bike. 'Let me congratulate you, love. He's quite a sexual athlete in the right company.'

As Sean got back behind the wheel, Kate asked, 'Is it OK if I come and sit in the front?'

'Fine by me.'

'I don't have to ask that fucking little shit for permission, do I?'

'You don't.'

He drove out of the service area, passing Patrick Brennan, raising a hand in ironic farewell.

Kate was determinedly silent while Eric gazed expressionlessly ahead.

'You really couldn't sink much lower, could you?'

'Needs must.'

Sean had the sudden urge to laugh and go on laughing. Kate was such a bloody cold fish. She'd got what she'd been working for, hadn't she? Now why couldn't she leave the poor sod alone?

'So you can exonerate Sean,' Eric explained.

'What on earth are you talking about?'

'If he was so ready and willing to bugger me, why did I start combing Estartit for callow youth?'

Kate didn't reply.

'After all, I went drinking with Sean, didn't I? I had every chance to screw him.'

'I just don't want to hear any more about your squalid little life.'

Eric closed his eyes. 'Wake me if any other creditors show up,' he said.

191

'What about a potential assassin?' asked Sean.

'Oh, you'll see him off. After all, you've had quite a bit of experience now.'

'Nothing very practical.'

'Don't worry. Survival's an instinct, isn't it?'

21

The Boeing was only half full as it taxied along the runway, and from his seat several rows behind Eric and Kate, Sean noticed their relationship had reached an even lower ebb as they studied the *Independent* and the *Guardian*, taking care not to communicate or even glance at each other. If the situation had not been so serious, there would have been something touching about their bizarre relationship. Suddenly he realised how isolated they both were, the steep-sided chasm yawning between them. A bridge, however improvised, seemed unlikely.

As the cabin crew prepared for take-off, Sean began to mull over what had occurred at the check-in.

Remembering almost too late that he still had the gun, he had whispered to Kate, 'What about your famous vanishing trick? Or shall I just drop the damn thing into one of those potted palms?'

'I've got a compartment in my bag that won't show up on the security screen.'

'Pure Bond?'

'Pure professionalism. So why don't you stop worrying?'

'So we won't be seeing each other again?'

'No.'

'Any chance of working for Midas?'

'Unlikely.'

'What about Eric?'

'He got a good price.'

'*Will* they come after us?'

'I've made sure of that.'

'*What*?' Sean was startled. He had thought the surprises – or at least the bulk of them – were over.

'Eric committed a cardinal sin.'

'Can't you tell me what it is?'

'Not here.'

'You despise him as much as ever?'

'In this case no.'

'Has he sinned against Midas?'

'He's wounded them.'

'Do they know what he's done?'

'I told them.'

Sean had felt a spurt of anger and frustration. Did she have to be so destructive? 'Why?'

She had shrugged. 'I wanted to wound him too. I thought we had a future. Then I realised I'd been wrong.'

Sean's thoughts had been in over-drive, trying to work out the permutations. The most glaring omission seemed to have been Midas's strategy. 'Why the hell did they even let Eric leave Estartit?'

'I persuaded them it would make more sense to let everything take its course until the plane was unloaded. I wanted to give him a chance.'

'I just don't get it. Surely they should have dealt with him immediately?'

'The decision was not to run any more risks.' Kate had been silent, watching Eric load the bags on to the belt. Then she had said, 'Maybe I should tell you that I was sorry Andrew screwed up.'

'And yet you stayed put after he died?'

'There was a lot to keep in place.'

'Until Eric was ready to be the sacrificial lamb.'

'Something like that.'

'How many other businesses have you given to Midas?'

'That's where the adrenalin came in.'

'And now?'

'It's all over. I'm just another Vi, another Auntie Liz. We all took Eric to the cleaners, one way or the other. But maybe the only person who learnt something was me.'

'Learnt what?'

'He made me realise what a shit I've become.' She had given Sean a wary glance. 'The worm,' Kate had said. 'It can turn . . .'

'Talking secrets?' Eric had asked as he had arrived with the boarding passes.

'We're sharing. Isn't that wonderful?'

*

194

'Give,' she had said and Sean had hastily dropped the automatic into what looked like a cloth-covered compartment in Kate's bag.

After a long time queuing at the baggage check which had almost broken Sean's nerve, the bag went on the conveyor belt, bumping through the rubber curtain and seeming to take an eternity emerging. Then, to their utter horror, one of the security team had picked it up, but as a colleague interrupted he pushed the bag away, absent-mindedly grabbing at another which, thankfully, mercifully, belonged to someone else.

Kate had hurriedly reclaimed her property and they had walked on as casually as they could manage. Sean had felt so weak, so damp with sweat, that he had hardly been able to put one foot in front of the other, amazed that they were proceeding unhindered to the plane.

'We're sharing.' Kate's voice had rung in his ears. 'Isn't that wonderful?'

Sean glanced round at his fellow passengers. Business people, a few holiday-makers, a clutch of women from a convention, a couple whispering to each other, a child travelling on his own, a man in a tracksuit. An anonymous enough collection, but at least one of them had to be aware of the extra cargo the Boeing was apparently carrying.

As the captain began to relay information about the weather, the height of the aircraft and the estimated time of arrival over the PA system, Sean picked up the in-flight magazine, idly leafing through the pages, already beginning to count each minute towards their arrival at Gatwick, the latest developments hammering away in his head. What had Eric done to damage Midas? Had it been planned and was there some kind of evidence that Sean might get hold of? And what about Kate's confession? Was that just another smoke-screen?

'Excuse me.'

A tall, elderly male passenger wearing a dark suit, clean-shaven, with a regimental tie, was hovering, looking as awkward as only an Englishman can when about to intrude.

'I've been asked to give up my seat.'

'Yes?'

'To a Muslim.' He now seemed deeply embarrassed.

'You have?'

'He has to face Mecca. Can I join you?'

'Of course,' Sean replied unwillingly.

He sat down next to him, and leant back in his seat. 'I really am grateful to you. I hope you don't mind.'

'Not at all.'

'I expect you were planning to spread out a bit. What a bore.'

'It's no problem.'

'The name's Fairley. Desmond Fairley.'

'Sean Pollard.'

'I hear it's raining in England.' Fairley opened a copy of the *Financial Times*. 'Still – I miss the old place. I couldn't live in the Med. The heat doesn't suit me. Now if I had more money . . .'

Sean groaned inwardly. With so much on his mind, was this guy really going to talk trivia all the way home to Gatwick?

'If only I had the Midas touch . . .'

Sean froze. 'Who?'

'Midas. Mythology, you know.' Fairley lowered his *Financial Times*. 'You're travelling with friends?'

'Yes.' Could he be a Farringdon contact? If not . . .

'There's been a bit of a cock-up.'

'In what way?'

'Mr Cole has been stupid.'

Sean didn't reply as his hopes plummeted.

'Stupid enough to record a confidential meeting.'

'What do you expect me to do? I'm only his driver.'

'We're not quite sure *who* you are. But for the moment I need the tape. I'd like you to retrieve it for me.'

'Surely Bradman can do that?'

'I'm very much afraid we've lost faith in her.'

'Why?'

'We think she could have been equally stupid.'

'What kind of tape are we talking about?'

'A micro. Rather on the small side.'

*

196

Sean suddenly wondered if he was the victim of an elaborate joke. Was Eric playing the game of his lifetime? But something about Fairley's manner convinced him that he wasn't.

They both had micro tapes. They were both insiders. But who was Eric working for? The shockwaves spread. Suppose Farringdon had run two agents? Just to be on the safe side.

Snap, cried Rik in a long-forgotten game. *Two Mr Bun the Baker*. And there was no disputing that.

Sean forced himself to remain as calm and as enigmatic as possible. Then he decided that a little aggression might be helpful. 'So Eric didn't let you take him to the cleaners after all? Are you saying Bradman's holding his hand?'

'We would like to think she has decided loyalty to Midas is more important. But people are unpredictable, aren't they?'

'I'm afraid I can't help you.'

'We'd be prepared to make an *ex gratia* payment.'

'Why do you think Bradman is being disloyal?'

'Familiarity breeds contempt. She's a long-time server.'

'Or maybe she finally regards the Midas touch with contempt.'

'We like to see our work as simply shifting the balance of power.'

'Like murdering Vi and Fred and – '

'I don't think we need an inquest.'

'So Bradman got herself a conscience at last?'

'I don't know anything about her conscience.'

'And you think Eric will pass across his tape? Just like that?'

'There are various approaches you might make.'

Was this a golden opportunity? His own tape was of little value compared with Eric's and Farringdon would regard its retrieval as the most glittering prize of all.

22

Kate was walking down the aisle towards them, carrying her bag.

Ignoring Fairley, she gave Sean an artificial smile. 'They'll be serving lunch soon. Feeling peckish, are you?'

'No champagne?'

'I don't think it's called for, do you?'

'I'm not sure about that.'

'One of these days,' she said slowly, 'we'll all go down together.' The smile became less artificial, almost warm, certainly inviting. Was it genuine, he wondered. Or was it the smile that had been the bait for the businesses? As Kate hurried on towards the toilets, Sean remembered that she had said those words before, but he couldn't remember when.

When Kate was out of earshot, Fairley began to negotiate again. 'I'm sure you're an ingenious man, Mr Pollard. If you extract the tape I'll give you two thousand pounds – in cash.' He sounded slightly uneasy.

'When?'

'On receipt.'

'You've got the money on you then?'

Fairley opened his briefcase and Sean saw that there were several stacks of banknotes.

'Do you always travel hopefully?'

'In my experience, petty cash can always come in useful.'

'Suppose I say your petty cash isn't quite enough?'

'I thought you might have that problem.'

'So?'

'You might like to work for my company. You'll find us generous employers. We're very diverse.'

'Lot of scope?'

'Oh – lots.'

Suddenly it was as if time was on hold again and Sean had the same disturbing split-second sensation he had had just before Vi and Fred had died, just as the despatch rider had driven up to the pumps. A flight attendant was frozen in mid-aisle, passengers were stock-still in their seats, and even the clouds looked as if they were painted on an unmoving horizon. Then normality returned in a flash as he remembered the resolve he had seen in Kate's eyes.

Sean got up.

'There's a good chap,' said Fairley appreciatively, and then gazed after him in gathering surprise as Sean hurried down the aisle in the opposite direction.

Every instinct told him that he could be too late. Why hadn't he realised before that she had reached such an impasse?

'Kate . . .'

She was just about to go into the toilet.

'What is it?' She turned to him reluctantly.

'We need to talk.'

'That's over now,' she said, sliding the door shut behind her.

'You were first,' said the middle-aged man in the tracksuit. indicating the vacant toilet opposite. 'That one's free now.'

'Sorry?' Sean stared at him uncomprehendingly and then glanced back. Eric was slumped in his seat, looking as if he was trying to sleep, and Fairley was engrossed in the *Financial Times*.

'Is anything wrong?' asked the man in the tracksuit.

Sean turned to the toilet door that Kate had just slammed shut and shouted her name. There was no reply.

'That lady . . .' he began.

'What about her?'

'She's ill. For Christ's sake. Help me break the door down.'

The man in the tracksuit was both disconcerted and disapproving. 'You'd better call a flight attendant,' he said as Sean put his shoulder to the door, but moved hurriedly back as he heard the dull thuds he had half expected to hear. 'Watch what you're doing. You had a drop too many? You know what the airlines are saying about drunks on – '

'Go back to your seat.'

'I'm in the queue – '

'You idiot.'

'I beg your pardon?'

The door blew open as Sean ran back down the aisle but the

blast caught the man in the tracksuit, sucking him out of the ragged hole that had opened up inside the toilet.

Could bullets have done all that damage, Sean wondered with all the objectivity of sudden loss. Or had she used something else?

Maybe her suicide wasn't spontaneous after all. Had Kate been planning to shoot Midas down for a long time? If so, why jeopardise the tape? Then Sean realised that Kate must have made a duplicate and stashed it somewhere a little safer than the crippled aircraft that would, in all probability, kill them all.

The Boeing was plunged into darkness with only emergency lighting illuminating the floor. Oxygen masks spiralled down from overhead as the plane shuddered and began to lose height. Cabin attendants made flurried attempts at reassurance but strangely there was hardly any panic. The passengers seemed transfixed, unable to believe they were involved in an impending disaster they would usually have associated with the movies – or even the newspapers where other people died in their millions, but never the reader.

'What did she do?' Eric gazed up in numbed disbelief.

'Shot herself.' Sean tried to remain on his feet as the aircraft began to plunge more sharply. 'She shot herself for Christ's sake – '

A flight attendant pushed past them. 'Get back in your seats, please.' She spoke brightly, as if they were experiencing mild turbulence. 'And make sure your seatbelts are fastened.'

Sean could hear her colleagues giving much the same instructions, and assuming the tannoy was down he grabbed at a dangling oxygen mask, took in a few breaths and then passed it to Eric who pushed the apparatus aside, standing up, dragging something wrapped in plastic from the pocket of his jeans.

'Take the tape and go and sit at the back. Apparently it's the best survival position.' He seemed calm, no longer dazed, fully in control.

'Come with me. Give yourself a chance.' Immediately he realised that was what he should have said to Kate.

'I've been working for Vi,' Eric confided. 'All the time. I've been loyal – doing what the old bitch would have wanted me to do. Now do what I tell you, for Christ's sake!'

'She'd have been proud of you.'

'The game's over.'

'What game?'

'Piss off, Sean. Do what I fucking tell you for once.'

He took the tape and stumbled back up the steeply inclined aisle, the fear biting for the first time, panic beginning to surge, particularly when he saw the blank looks in the eyes of the passengers, still unable to accept what was happening to them.

Some of the overhead compartments had burst open and bags had already fallen and were lying in the aisle. As Sean struggled over them he saw a stream of white powder trickling down to the floor. Pure heroin, he thought. The ultimate oblivion.

'What's that?' asked an elderly man. 'It looks like snow. Is it snowing outside?' He seemed a child again.

'We're going to make an emergency landing. Why don't you come and sit at the back with me? It might be safer there.'

He shook his head. 'I'm with my wife. We must stay together. We don't want to make a fuss.'

Sean walked on up the aisle, moved by the old man's self-effacement, his innate desire not to make a nuisance of himself, to remain loyal – but passive – in his love and protection.

The superstructure of the Boeing was now making a terrifying grinding sound as if it was about to break up, and most of the passengers had their heads down in the brace position. As the plane flew out of cloud, Sean could see distant fields and a long, winding river below.

Fairley, still holding his *Financial Times*, was gazing ahead, no longer interested in Eric Cole's betrayal.

Sean struggled on until he found a seat at the back of the aircraft. He sat down and strapped himself in. The in-flight magazine hung out of the rack by his knees and the cover picture depicted a young and handsome actor. Underneath, the caption read, 'Jacob Fern is in love with life'.

*

201

'Brace!' shouted a cabin attendant. 'Brace now.'

The passengers were still largely silent. No one spoke. No one even attempted to cry out and Sean could only hear the occasional whimper. Someone prayed softly.

'God be in my head, and in my understanding.'

Sean saw Abbie, Rik and Mary getting into the car outside the front gate of the house.

'God be in my eyes, and in my looking.'

Now he was driving.

'We won't stay long, will we?' asked Mary.

'Until after tea.'

'That *is* long, Mum.'

'We've come a long way.'

'I don't like Henry,' complained Rik. 'He's a wanker.'

'God be in my mouth, and in my speaking.'

Vi and Fred and Elizabeth and Kate. In his previous incarnation Sean would never have known such people. Now it was as if they had never existed. Sean and Danny. Colliding worlds in a flying coffin.

'God be in my heart, and in my thinking.'

'Why are we going, Mum?' asked Rik aggressively.

'Because Ann's my cousin. She likes to see us.'

'We've already seen them twice this year.'

'Look,' Danny had intervened, the anger sparking again, 'why don't you two try to do something for *us* for a change?'

'We have,' said Mary indignantly.

'What?'

'We tidied our rooms last night.'

'God be at my end and at my departing.'

Sean looked out of the window. He had always watched landings while most other people averted their eyes. Now he was gazing down at the river running through the water meadows, seeing ploughed fields and miles of moorland. Were they going to come down here?

He remembered the weir, gazing down into the dark water and then feeling Eric grip his ankles. Life is precious. Life is sweet.

The Boeing had almost straightened up again, the steep dive controlled, the cabin less cold as they neared the ground.

Suddenly he saw Eric get up and turn towards him. He was smiling.

Below, the river and meadows no longer belonged to a toy landscape. Instead they were menacingly real.

Somehow, at the last minute, the pilot brought up the nose of the Boeing, skimming a ploughed field as the stricken aircraft fluttered, the landing gear disabled. He's too short. The thought raged. He's flying too short.

Some lines of George Borrow, learnt at school and forgotten since, permeated Sean's agony and brought a measure of peace.

> There's night and day, brother, both sweet things;
> Sun, moon, and stars, brother, all sweet things;
> There's likewise a wind on the heath.
> Life is very sweet, brother;
> Who would wish to die?

I've run a crooked mile, said a voice in his head.

'Wonder if they got any doughnuts?' asked Vi. Where? In heaven? Did she deserve the pearly gates? Or had she descended to the underworld? 'Toasted will do,' she added grudgingly.

The copse of trees reared up and for a split second Sean could make out some kind of growth on the trunks.

Then the noise of violently disintegrating metal was all-embracing and his ears were filled with a rending, tearing sound. Suddenly something hit him between the shoulder blades.

Darkness came.

Part Four

DANNY AGAIN

23

Farringdon sat beside Danny's bed.

'Same hospital,' he said. 'Fortunately not the same injuries.'

'The second time Eric's saved my life.'

'I don't think the back of any aircraft is conclusively proven to be the safest place.'

'He never conclusively proved anything.'

'I'm not so sure. What about the tape? He did Vi proud.'

'Has Midas been blown apart?' asked Danny.

'They've been badly damaged and we're arresting some prominent people.'

'Sixty dead. Forty-one survivors. But so far there's nothing about the heroin in the press.'

'There won't be. We've put out a D notice, mainly because a member of the Cabinet's involved.' Farringdon glanced curiously at the tulip curtains. 'I remember those. Surely to God they didn't put you back in the same bed?'

'There's this nurse. Ana. She wanted to look after me.'

'Is that allowed?'

'She doesn't play by the book.'

'So you're going home? Can you bear that?'

'It had to happen some time.'

'What about being Danny?'

'He'll be a bit of a stranger to me.'

'Eric was buried yesterday. Next to his parents.'

'Fred would have been pleased. Vi would be furious. Even nailing Midas wouldn't make up for losing the business. What about Elizabeth?'

'She's helping with our enquiries.'

'Did she plea-bargain?'

'You can say that again. But she's really only a minor player. Your real coup was Midas. They'll regroup of course, but you hit them hard.'

'What about Gatwick?'

'There won't be many arrests and I'm sure Midas will pull out anyway. We showed we've got muscle. That's the important thing, and this is the first breakthrough we've had.'

'So I'm redundant. What do I do? Lick my wounds and crawl back to the Met?'

'When you've had a long rest, I'd like you to consider the teaching profession. I know a private school in a cathedral town with a paederast ring that's as complex as Midas. Their tentacles are everywhere.' Farringdon got to his feet. 'Going home is going to be your toughest assignment for the moment.'

'At least I haven't got Sean to fight.'

'Wasn't it Danny who had the problem?'

He drove back to The Oaks in a rented car.

Pulling up outside, he waited for a long time before he had the strength to get out. But once he was standing by his garden gate, Danny felt a little more resolved, particularly when he noticed the grass needed cutting.